Also by Barbara Wilson

Pam Nilsen Mysteries:
Murder in the Collective
Sisters of the Road

Other Works:
Gaudí Afternoon
Ambitious Women
Cows and Horses
Miss Venezuela

THE
DOG COLLAR
MURDERS

Barbara Wilson

Seal Press

Library of Congress Cataloging-in-Publication Data
Wilson, Barbara, 1950-
  The dog collar murders / Barbara Wilson.
    p.   cm.
  ISBN 1-878067-25-7 :
  I. Title.
  PS3573.I45678D64   1989
813'.54—dc19   88-27016
                                                                    CIP

Cover design: Kris Morgan
Printed in the United States of America
First edition, March 1989
10 9 8 7 6 5 4 3

for Wendy Smith

Acknowledgements

This novel was written in England, where I benefited from discussions with British feminists as well as from a new perspective on the American porn wars. I'd especially like to thank Sue O'Sullivan and Linda Semple for reading the manuscript; Jen Green, Leslie Winegrad and Barbara Gunnell for material and emotional support; and Ann Coppel for technical information. Abundant thanks to Faith Conlon, the best editor and friend a feminist crime writer could hope for.

The Dog Collar Murders

"But more important was the multiplication of discourses concerning sex in the field of exercise of power itself: an institutional incitement to speak about it, and to do so more and more; a determination on the part of the agencies of power to hear it spoken about, and to cause it to speak through explicit articulation and endlessly accumulated detail."

Michel Foucault, *The History of Sexuality, Volume 1*

1

WHEN PENNY AND I were eight years old she went through a wedding phase. She used to like to get dressed up in some old lace curtains and to pretend she was getting married. Not to anyone in particular, just married.

I was supposed to hold up the train and catch the flowers afterwards.

Twenty-two years later Penny was doing it in earnest. If this had been one of those novels we used to read or one of the stories Penny used to tell me, then I should have been the happiest girl on earth now—my twin sister was getting married to the man she loved and I was the brides-maid.

Of course, some things weren't quite the way we might have imagined them. Instead of a white lace dress and gossamer veil Penny was wearing an embroidered blouse and a handwoven skirt from Guatemala, and instead of tossing me a bouquet after the ceremony she handed me her baby, so she could kiss the groom.

I kissed the groom too—after all, he'd been my lover once for nearly two years—and Penny kissed my partner ("On the mouth!" Hadley said later), then I kissed Penny and handed baby Antonia back to her, and we all trooped

3

out of the house into the garden for the reception.

It was late September. The leaves of the horse chestnut trees were the color of marigolds. The vegetable garden hadn't been turned over yet, and there were still squash vines and tomato plants warming themselves in the afternoon light. Around the borders were dahlias, my mother's dahlias, and roses in full bloom. The sky was a faint but very fresh blue and the air had that wonderful fall clarity, that is partly a fragrance of something ending.

Hadley came up behind me and put her arms around my waist. Her hair smelled good, of fall and herb shampoo, and she was wearing a new light wool jacket that rubbed pleasantly on my bare arms.

"Always a bridesmaid, never a groom," she said.

"It's all so reactionary," I muttered, while smiling at the arriving guests, and directing them to the happy pair. "If *I* were the one getting married—to you, for instance—do you think all these people, all these relatives and friends of the family, would be turning up? No way."

"Some of them don't seem too pleased to see that Penny has an eight-week-old baby at her breast," Hadley noted. "I think the baby's supposed to be a gentle swelling under the bride's dress, so people can gossip and speculate."

It probably *was* the first time many of the guests had congratulated a bride who was breastfeeding even as she shook their hands. Ray hovered around her, ethnic in an embroidered white shirt and with his black hair brilliantined, the image of the proud husband and father. Who would have suspected this side of him even three years ago, when we'd both been experts on shared birth control? Who would have suspected, as we quarreled about the merits of diaphragm vs. condom, that today we'd be standing here, related, me the lesbian sister of his wife, him the father of my niece? We exchanged a shy glance from time to time—our anger at each other had been transmuted into an ironic and bemused sort of tenderness. Penny was the one I was mad at—for reasons I hesitated to examine too

4

deeply.

The afternoon passed quickly. My lesbian friends came and were respectfully sarcastic, but I hardly had time to joke with them and hear their commiserations. I was too busy helping be the hostess at this house where Penny and I had grown up, where Penny and Ray and baby Antonia lived now. There were so many people to talk to: the Mortensens from down the street, Aunt Hilda who had come from Everett with her docile husband George, Uncle Walt from Minnesota with his wife Ingrid and their son the fourteen-year-old computer genius. There were Ray's illustrious parents, Doctors Hiyamoto and Contrerez, who had flown in from the UNICEF station in Bangladesh. June Jasper, our long time co-worker at the print shop and Penny's best friend, was here with her boyfriend Eddy (*she* didn't think she had to get married, did she?) and her two girls Ade and Amina. There were friends from different stages of our lives—from grade school, high school, the university, from various political groups that had once taken up hours of our time—the Tenants' Union, Crabshell Anti-Nuclear Alliance, Seattle Abortion Rights. . . .

There were new friends too. Zee, a Filipina who was studying filmmaking at USC and had flown up for the day. Beth and Janis, friends of mine from last winter; they'd brought Trish, who was now a junior at an alternative school and doing well. There were also new political comrades of Penny and Ray's, people who'd gone to pick coffee beans with them in Nicaragua last January, as well as our newest worker at the printshop, Moe, and his lover, Allen.

The garden was filled with people. "Penny looks so lovely," said Mrs. Mortensen. "Your mother would have been so pleased."

I could only nod and smile and move away with the excuse of getting another tray of hors d'oeuvres from the kitchen. I was stopped halfway to the house by Beth.

"Look over there, isn't that Loie Marsh?" Beth gestured to a small but growing group near the porch.

"What's she doing back in town, I wonder?"

I looked. It was definitely Chloe—or Loie, as she was usually called—Marsh. Ten years ago she'd been the putative head of the women against violence against women contingent here in Seattle. I remembered going to a slide show she gave right before a Women Take Back the Night march—it was the famous presentation, with the slide from *Hustler* of the woman going into the meatgrinder and coming out as hamburger. Loie had roused us all to fury.

Soon after, it had been eight or nine years ago now, she'd left Seattle for Boston, where she wrote a famous book against pornography, *The Silenced Heart*, and organized a number of conferences, panels and speak-outs. Since then she'd been a featured speaker on TV talk shows and the college circuit, an anti-porn celebrity.

"She apparently came back to Seattle to write another book," Miranda, an old friend, said, overhearing us. "She's been telling people she's broke and exhausted. She's staying with her cousin Hanna Sandbakker, the actress."

Hanna Sandbakker had been with Penny and Ray in Nicaragua—that must be why they'd invited her and Loie. I didn't really know Hanna myself, though I'd seen her a number of times on Seattle stages. She was a willowy woman with a mane of ash-blond hair, known for her tragic roles in Ibsen and Strindberg. Her trademark was a velvety voice with a slight catch that could make even the most banal words sound remarkable. I especially remembered her as Hedda Gabler, with her pistols.

"Loie's not just sitting around though," Miranda went on. "She's one of the main speakers at the porn conference next week. I already know what she's going to say—she's telling everyone around her now. She thinks the women's movement has been invaded and betrayed by a bunch of sexual liberals, 'so-called feminists' and sadomasochists."

"Surely she makes some distinction?" Hadley asked ironically. She had come up and was holding a tray of champagne and Calistoga.

"There isn't one to people like Loie," Miranda said.

"Saying you're against censorship is practically like saying you like to tie people up and whip them until they bleed."

Everyone laughed nervously, and I looked over at Loie. She was a tall woman, five ten or eleven, with large bones, big hands and feet. Her face was interesting, but not particularly attractive; there was something smooth and slightly convex about it, like the lid of an enamel saucepan. Her short curly blond hair was brushed back tightly over her shiny forehead. Like her cousin she had a particularly distinctive voice; I couldn't catch the words from here, but I heard the cadence, rhetorical and seductive.

She had gathered around her a small eager group of our guests. Hanna was off holding baby Antonia and chatting with Penny, but there were six or seven others listening to Loie speak. With some discomfort I noticed that Elizabeth Ketteridge had turned up at the reception and was standing next to Loie Marsh, apparently drinking in her words. A small woman with big eyes, very little hair and enormous hoop earrings, she was a counselor who dealt with survivors of rape and sexual abuse. I had gotten to know her earlier this year.

"Well, if that's the case, let's hope that Miko and Loie don't run into each other then," someone laughed.

Kimiko Lewis was a local video artist who had recently taken up the cause of lesbian sexual explicitness. She was forever attempting to show her videos at local film festivals and bookstores.

"Is Miko here?"

"No," I said. "I hope not anyway. That woman really gets on my nerves."

"That's 'cause she asked me to be in one of her sex movies," said Hadley, preening.

"You said no, I hope, Hadley," Beth smiled.

"Of course," Hadley sighed. "She didn't offer me near enough money."

"Well, we'll all have a chance to see Miko and Loie square off soon. They're both on one of the panels at the porn conference," Miranda said.

"Is that really what it's called?" someone passing by asked. "I've seen posters around, but I thought the conference was the 'Seattle Conference on Sexuality.'"

Miranda laughed. "Right. So for some people it's the sex conference. For others it's the porn conference. Watch the fireworks!"

It wasn't exactly that I was having a *bad* time. If it had just been a social reunion I would have enjoyed myself immensely. But it was a wedding reception, one of the important markers society uses to separate the socially acceptable from the socially unacceptable. Penny and I had been arguing about it for weeks.

"What's wrong with just living together the way you've been doing?" I'd said. "You can make legal and financial arrangements just the same—better even, because then you can be conscious of what you're doing."

"I'm through living with people. I want this to be different, to show I'm really committed to the relationship."

"Great. How do you think that makes me feel? I'm in a relationship too. If marriage is the only way to show commitment where does that leave us?"

"Well, you could get married if you wanted—I mean, they have ceremonies, don't they?. . . You, I mean."

"You know goddamn well a ritual for lesbians or gay men isn't the same thing as a wedding. If Hadley and I got married, I wouldn't automatically become Mrs. Pam Nilsen-Harper, respectable supporter of the status quo."

She got defensive. "We're only doing it because of the baby. . . "

"The baby's got nothing to do with it. You're only doing it because you want to and because you want to be like everyone else. You're just like the rest of those feminists who go to Nicaragua and come back idealizing marriage and the family."

"Everybody's not a lesbian, you know," Penny snarled, falling into the kind of jargon she would have es-

8

chewed a year ago. "How could a population like Nicaragua replace itself if everyone were? Sexual preference is the product of an advanced capitalist consumer society."

"Oh give me a break, you Sandinista robot," I'd said and stormed out of the house. And then I'd sat in my car and sobbed like a fool. Ever since Antonia had been born, on the second of August, I'd been an emotional wreck. Up to then it had all been interesting. I'd gone with Penny to the doctor and the birth clinic. I'd learned to do the breathing exercises with her so I could be the back-up coach during the birth. I'd sat around with Penny and Ray, tossing names back and forth. I'd finally moved all my stuff out of my old room into the basement and helped paint it yellow and white. And when Penny had called me at three in the morning I'd told her how much I loved her and had raced over to Group Health to be there with her. My twin sister was having a baby!

Ray and I were with her the whole time; we laughed and wept and breathed and struggled with her. And after it was over I held Antonia in my arms and thought she was the most beautiful creature I'd ever seen.

I don't know what happened after that. It was as if I had post-partum blues instead of Penny. While she learned to change diapers and bathe the baby, while she and Ray discussed the color and consistency of Antonia's stools and what position it was best to burp her from, I felt increasingly miserable and left out. And when they started talking about marriage I began to freak out.

"I don't understand why you're so upset," Hadley tried to reason with me.

"She wants to get married, Hadley! She's going to do the whole thing—a husband and a baby!"

"Think of it as having more relatives," she offered, but that just made me cry. For some reason I had begun to miss my parents very badly again this year, even though they had been gone for almost five years.

Hadley tried again, "You're just different people, Pam.

9

You want different things."

"It's the principle, Hadley," I said. "Society's going to reward her now. I'll never be rewarded. I'm going to be punished my whole life. She should have stuck with me—out of solidarity."

Hadley sighed. "If you'd been a lesbian as long as I had, Pam honey, you would have given up wanting to be acceptable a long time ago. You need to work on accepting yourself."

But Hadley didn't have a twin sister.

Late in the evening, after helping Penny and Ray clear up, Hadley and I returned to the houseboat on Portage Bay that we'd been subletting for the past two months. We put on our sweaters and down vests, for it was quite cool, and sat out on the floating dock, drinking jasmine scented tea and watching the lights of the bridge and the university opposite us on the dark water.

It was a way we'd had of being together for weeks now; a day didn't feel complete until we'd gone out and surveyed the evening colors and discussed the weather and the temperature. We sat there now, companionably, not talking, just drinking tea and looking.

Hadley and I had now been a couple for almost eight months; the first six we'd lived apart but spent increasing amounts of time together. We'd been happy and hadn't ever talked about living together. But when Peggy and Denise asked if we'd be interested in subletting the houseboat while they took advantage of Peggy's grant for traveling in South America, both Hadley and I eagerly said yes.

It was living together without really living together. It's just for three months, we said. Still, we'd each given up our apartments and so far hadn't made any plans for what to do when Peggy and Denise came back at the end of October. The problem was that living together had raised more questions than it had answered for us: how close did we want to be; were we strictly monogamous; was this a relationship made in heaven that would last forever or just your usual two year lesbian romance?

The houseboat was small and very shipshape, a rectangle divided ingeniously into different spaces for eating and sleeping and entertaining. Hadley's problem was her height; she kept knocking into the bedroom ceiling the first week. I had trouble with the rocking of the boat in the beginning; my legs felt wobbly on land and I had also been awakened on more than one occasion in the first two weeks by waves that made the center beam of the houseboat crack like a whip. I didn't like strange noises at night, and would often wake up with my heart in my mouth, hearing the creaking of the dock alongside the boat and imagining that someone was coming to get me.

It was a comfort to have Hadley; yet even she had to put up with a lot. All summer I'd been taking self-defense classes; I took them so seriously that they entered into my dreams. I felt constantly prepared for attack. Once when we first moved into the houseboat and I'd gone to bed early, Hadley got quietly into bed, casually threw an arm over my shoulder, and nestled close to me. Almost without waking I threw her off on to the floor.

Now we sat cuddling on the deck, watching how the lights reddened the water so festively. I loved the Portage Bay side of Lake Union—it was more relaxed and informal. Lake Union was a working lake, full of tugs and barges, views obscured by masts and sails. Portage Bay seemed quieter, a place where kayakers, canoeists and windsurfers could play. And sometimes, surprisingly, it was utterly calm, like tonight. Not a boat in sight; it was as if we sat by the side of a lake in the mountains.

"It was funny to see Loie," Hadley said eventually. "So much of that porn debate seems to happen on the east coast. You tend to feel that out here people don't get so involved, so caught up in it all."

"That's true," I said, taking off my glasses and resting my head on her shoulder. "I hardly even know what I think about the whole thing. Do you?"

"No," she said. "Not really. It's been years since I've been certain. I mean, I've read on both sides of the issue, but it's as if the passion of each position negates the other—so when I'm reading someone like Dworkin I sometimes think, yes, she's absolutely right: pornography is about male power, it's a strategy of subordination. But when I read someone else on the other side I think, no, pornographic imagery and sexism aren't always the same thing. We need to keep them distinct, and as women, especially as women, we need to keep our options open to explore our sexuality."

She sighed and looked out across the water. "Maybe after the conference next week I'll have a better grasp of the current thinking. Maybe there's some way to hold both views—some way to understand the contradictions. . . . "

"Yeah," I said and stared at the black waves outlined in silver that came towards us steadily. "You know, though, Hadley, I really *wish* she hadn't gotten married."

2

I WOKE UP EARLY THE next morning and went out on the floating dock. The bay was like a mirror trying to come awake. There were hardly any individual ripples or waves; instead the whole body of water seemed to be in movement, a shivery, massive kind of movement, as if it were stirring from the bottom. It was a gray morning, but it didn't matter by the water, where everything was so luminescent. This morning the sky was like torn bits of very absorbent watercolor paper, with dark gray seeping or branching onto the silver-white color.

It was Sunday and it was bound to get busier on the lake. Now there were only a few solitary scullers from the university speeding along the surface of the water like dragonflies. Later the pleasure boats would come out, the big cruisers full of festive rich people who would steer dangerously close to the docks and would look in the windows. If caught, they'd remark sheepishly, "Nice weather we're having!"

But Hadley and I had learned to ignore them, and to go about our business openly—or to close the curtains when we couldn't. Houseboat life was different than other sorts of life. In part you felt far from Seattle with no traffic, no people in the street; out here on the end of the dock the nearest neighbor was the houseboat in back, the one over to the side. Yet it was also a strangely active, peopled world: imagine living in a regular house, on the second floor, and looking out your window to see people flying past, silent and smiling.

I was feeling good this morning, good about myself, good about Hadley. Since she'd come back into my life, meaning had returned to everyday events, and it looked like she was here to stay, after finally getting her father into a nursing home in Texas. For one thing she was in business now, no longer working in the graphic trades like me, but the owner of a thriving, if odd, little concern.

The family fortunes in Houston had declined for the last few years to a frightening degree. Hadley told stories of whole neighborhoods in the city with FOR SALE signs out in front. She didn't suffer as much as some of her family or their friends—for a long while she'd had her money invested in a variety of socially responsible causes and businesses—but with the recent fluctuations in the stock market, she noted a definite drop in income. She decided at that point to put her remaining capital into a business idea she'd had for a while.

She opened what she called the Espressomat, a combination laundromat and espresso cafe, on Capitol Hill. Not the most likely—or genteel, as some of her family might have said—of ventures, but it was a lot safer than the stock market these days, and from its opening a month ago it had been a great success.

You had to admit it was a new concept: that people who ccouldn't afford or didn't have room for washers and dryers had a right to get their clothes clean in surroundings that weren't completely disgusting and filthy.

"I've never understood," Hadley had said to the newspaper reporter who interviewed her for a big feature story in *The Post-Intelligencer* ("Coffee and Clean Clothes Spell Success for Houston Heiress"), "why laundromats in general and those in the inner cities in particular have to be so downbeat and humiliating. At any one time a quarter to a third of the machines aren't working, the dryers either don't dry or they turn your clothes into potato chips. And if you don't have a car and can't just drop the clothes off, you're stuck either sitting there trying to read in one of those plastic molded chairs with gum stuck all over it and forced to listen to a pop station turned up as loud as it will go, or you're driven out in search of some store to browse in or a cafe to sit in. So I thought—why not make it easy for people? Why not make it nice? Everybody's got to wash clothes. So why not make it fun?"

So Hadley had. The Espressomat had become two businesses, really; to cut down on the noise and to conform with licensing laws, she'd created two separate spaces with separate entrances and a door between them. The cafe part resounded to the hiss of the elaborate copper espresso machine and the buzz of animated conversations, while the washers and dryers next door chugged along purposefully (being too new to have begun to break down yet). The combined smell of French Roast and Tide was a little unusual and, I thought, a little too strong. Still, I was getting used to it.

Good thing too, since I was spending quite a lot of my free time there.

Hadley had gotten up and she came out on deck with a cup of coffee. She was dressed in Levis and an inarticulate blue tee-shirt. Her shoulder-length silvery hair was pulled back into a ponytail and her blue-green eyes were awake and glad.

"Brrr—you can feel it's starting to get to be fall now in the mornings, can't you?"

The sun had come out now and the weathered gray wood of the deck was warming slightly. Where the sun shone on the water there was a pattern of diamonds, small, flashing bits of light.

Hadley went on, "You know, we really *are* going to have to decide soon what to do in November."

"November!" I said, even though I knew she was

right. "It's still September, for godssakes. According to the calendar it's still summer."

"Next week is October 1st," she said inexorably. "And there are so many things we haven't talked about."

"I know, I know," I said, to head her off from spoiling this beautiful morning with talk of househunting, boundaries, other women, and the future in general. "And I *want* to talk, of *course* I want to talk—but I think we should set aside some *real* time for it." I had learned this strategy in collective meetings.

"Okay," said Hadley equably, but she sighed. "Only let's not leave it too long... I have some ideas. . . . "

"Next week!" I said. "Next week, I promise."

"All right," she said. "Next week."

Later in the morning we "stopped by" the Espressomat. Even though Hadley had three full- and two part-time employees, she was putting in long hours herself. The Espressomat was open from seven in the morning to eleven at night, seven days a week.

Today both sections of the place were full and the steady hum of the washers and dryers underlay the rattling of cups and saucers.

I picked up part of *The New York Times*, Hadley made me a frothy decaf mocha and I sat down in a corner, underneath a poster from *The Threepenny Opera*. After a while, two women I knew came in, Debi and Sarah. They weren't washing their clothes; it was purely social.

We chatted generally for a while and then the conversation turned, as it had the day before at the reception, to the sexuality/pornography conference next week.

"I'm really looking forward to hearing Loie Marsh speak," said Debi. "She's been one of my heroes for years."

"Me too," said Sarah. "I remember when I read *The Silenced Heart*. It just blew me away. It expressed so many things about men and living in a male world that I had just

16

taken for granted."

"They don't write books like that anymore," agreed Debi. "Really groundbreaking books like that."

I hadn't read it, just like I had never managed to read *The Female Eunuch, Future Shock* and Carlos Castenada. No good reason—I just happened to be reading something else at the time and then the historical moment passed. I said, "I wonder why Loie hasn't written anything else since then?"

"She's probably too busy going around speaking. I saw her on Phil Donahue once. She was fabulous. It must have been—five years ago?"

"What else is going on at the conference?" I asked. I still hadn't decided if I wanted to go. From the corner of my eye I watched Hadley pouring a stream of hot milk into a row of cups. She was concentrating hard, a furrow between her brows. She'd once told me that waitressing was the hardest job in the world.

Debi pulled out a flyer. "There are some really interesting workshops: here's one on the Green River murders, another on legal aspects of censorship, something on sexist images of women in the media, Elizabeth Ketteridge talking about use of pornography by rapists and child molesters, lots of others. And in the evening there's going to be a panel discussion: Loie Marsh, Gracie London, Elizabeth Ketteridge, Kimiko Lewis and some woman named Sonya Gustafson from Christians Against Pornography. What a line-up."

"I heard," said Sarah, lowering her voice, "that some S/M women wanted to present a workshop. But the organizers refused." She nodded over in the direction of two women who were sitting quietly reading *The Seattle Times* in an alcove under a poster of Marlene Dietrich in *The Blue Angel*. "Those are two of the main ones, the main S/Mers—Nicky Kay and Oak on the left."

My gaze covertly followed hers. The women looked perfectly ordinary. The one called Nicky Kay was small, with a rather athletic body and a pleasant, nondescript face; glasses, brown curly hair. She was wearing a crisp striped shirt and jeans. Oak, if that was really her name, was taller, with a head that seemed slightly too big for her body. It made her look a little wobbly somehow. She was wearing a leather vest over a white tee-shirt and heavy boots. Otherwise, she didn't look too threatening.

But Debi and Sarah obviously found them both very threatening. They began to whisper: "orgy chambers... dog collars with spikes... Mary said... hot dripping wax... and *nipple* clamps!"

I knew, of course, that there were lesbian sadomasochists around, but I had never paid them much attention. A few years ago, in Seattle, as in San Francisco and a few other cities, there'd been something of an uproar, but it had died down and even radical feminists seemed to have resigned themselves to its presence in the community. I'd heard it said that Seattle was an S/M mecca of sorts, but it didn't intersect much with my world.

"I heard that Nicky Kay supports herself and Oak by dancing downtown at the Fun Palace."

"Really?" I couldn't quite picture it. She looked so... well, quiet.

But Debi and Sarah's attention had been diverted by the entrance of someone else into the cafe. "Now, there's a character! At least Nicky and Oak keep a low profile."

Miko Lewis had never kept a low profile in her life. She bounced in wearing tight black stretch pants calligraphed with neon pink, a black bustier underneath a flowing, pink silk shirt. Her spikey black hair had been bleached white on the tips and her rough complected face exuded joyous energy.

"Hadley! How's my favorite Texan today?" She hopped on to one of the chairs at the counter and leaned over so (I imagined) Hadley could get a good look at her thrusting cleavage. "Steam me up a double, darling. I've got a heavy day of editing sex scenes ahead."

Hadley laughed good-naturedly. "So when are we going to get to see some of these famous lesbian sex videos?"

18

"At the moment I'm only giving private screenings," she drawled in a low voice that was nonetheless audible to everyone in the room.

Debi and Sarah looked at me sympathetically, and I flushed. But just as I was thinking about going over and pushing her off her stool, Miko (who had certainly been aware of my presence all along), turned casually and said, "Oh hi, Pam. You come along too. A week from this Thursday night, my studio."

She downed the espresso in one gulp, slapped a dollar on the counter and, with a wave, flung herself out the door. Someone applauded.

"She doesn't just make stupid videos," was all I could mutter. "She fucking thinks she's in one."

That evening we went to Penny and Ray's for dinner. Ray and Hadley decided to take Antonia for a little stroll in the park while there was still some light. They may have thoughtfully been giving Penny and me some time to talk. Or, more likely, a chance to get in a good fight before dinner.

We worked well together usually and tonight was no exception. We moved around the kitchen, Penny making vegetable ratatouille, me whipping up a lemon mousse for dessert. I tried not to feel that everything was strange and different between us. I'd lived in this house much of my life and inherited it with Penny when our parents died. Now Penny lived here with a baby and a husband and was talking about buying my share of the house.

"It's only fair," she said. "You'll want to have a house of your own... "

"I like what you're doing with the windows," I interrupted. "I never did like those curtains."

"I hated to get rid of them. Somehow their pattern reminded me of being a kid and eating dinner in the kitchen. But they were falling apart. These blinds are much better."

She returned to her subject. "Are things okay with Hadley? Are you going to move in together after the experiment with the houseboat? You know, we need to get this house settled and then you could think about buying something together... "

"We're not that far along," I cut Penny off. Inside I was vaguely aware that it pissed me off that she seemed to think the house belonged to her. "So far living together seems like a vacation. Both of us have a lot of things in boxes. We're living in someone else's space. It's fun, but it's not real life."

"Oh, I think it will work out," she said encouragingly. "I think you should think about buying a house together."

I tried to switch the topic to something innocuous. "So, are you going to that all day workshop on pornography/sexuality—whatever it is—this Saturday?"

"The one with Loie and Gracie and everybody, you mean? I don't know. I might try to go to the panel discussion in the evening. I'll probably skip the workshops. I've got to do some work for the Nicaragua benefit next month. I said I'd work on the mailing."

"The conference will probably be interesting... "

"Yeah, maybe." Penny paused. "To tell the truth, pornography seems like such a middle-class white issue to me. When people all over the world are struggling just to get enough to eat, much less retain some individual freedoms, it's pretty weird when countries like America are so obsessed with defining under what conditions attractive naked bodies can be displayed."

I was silent.

"And no, I'm not turning into some kind of Marxist hardliner. I don't like seeing pictures of women being objectified for sale in every convenience store any more than you do. But compared to people getting murdered every day for their beliefs—well, all I'm saying is that for most of us porn is a kind of intellectual debate about civil liberties."

I couldn't help it. "Porn isn't intellectual," I said. "Of

all the millions of discussions in feminism, porn is about the least intellectual. It's physical, it's about bodies. It's not about speech, unless men can only speak using women's bodies."

"I'm sorry, but I don't think men are the problem." Penny turned away coldly. "And I don't know why every conversation with you has to turn into some kind of lesbian lecture."

"Well, I feel like I'm in some kind of indoctrination camp when I'm with you. Six weeks in Nicaragua! You'd think you were with Mao on the Long March! Some radical you are—I'm about a thousand times more radical than you are in the way I live my life."

"Oh, now we're going to talk about the wedding, aren't we? I knew it was going to come around to that. I knew that's what you really wanted to talk about."

"You're crazy if you think I want to talk about your wedding. That's the last thing I want to discuss—talk about bourgeois issues!"

"What's a bourgeois issue?" said Ray mildly, coming in with Hadley and Antonia. He was carrying Antonia in a backpack and they all looked fresh-cheeked and healthy after their walk in the park.

"Marriage!"

"Pornography!"

Antonia began to cry and Penny snatched her up and started to feed her. The sight of her maternal breast was like an insult in the present circumstances and I put my head into the refrigerator to check the lemon mousse and to cool off.

"Poor little thing," Hadley said and I think she meant Antonia. "Let's hope they've resolved some of this before you grow up."

3

THE SEXUALITY CONFERENCE was structured so that there were slots for two workshops in the morning and two in the afternoon, each an hour and a half long with an hour for lunch. At four-thirty there were to be two closing speeches, the first by Gracie London on "A Decade of a Single-Issue Politics—Time to Move On?" and the second by Loie Marsh: "Sexual Liberalism—the Death of Feminism?" In spite of the question marks there seemed little doubt which way the speakers leaned and what conclusions they were expecting to draw.

There were to be about twelve different workshops, some given twice. They ranged from "Current Research on the Effects of Pornography" to "Sex Workers Speak Out," from "Whose Sexual Revolution Was It, Anyway?" to "Sexist Images in the Media—More Dangerous Than Porn?" There were workshops on sexual abuse and bisexuality, on safe sex and the politics of disabled women's sexuality. The nearest the organizers had gotten to the S/M controversy was the workshop/video presentation entitled, "Is It Porn When a Lesbian Makes It?" given by Kimiko Lewis. The organizers had also stayed away from the Christian element in the planning of the confer-

22

ence, though they had invited Sonya Gustafson of Christians Against Pornography to speak that evening at the public panel with Loie, Gracie, Elizabeth and Miko.

The conference was being held at Catholic-owned Seattle University and was well-attended, albeit by most of the usual feminist crowd and a few earnest-looking students. Hadley and I split up immediately. She headed off for Loie Marsh's workshop on the history of the anti-pornography movement because she was curious to hear this woman everybody had been talking so much about, while I decided to begin on solid footing with the current research workshop.

"Miko's talk is at ten-thirty," Hadley said as we parted. "It'll probably be packed."

"Ummm."

"She's not really so bad, you know. She just likes attention."

"Yes, that's obvious. But I'm still not impressed."

"See you at lunch then?"

I nodded and she went off. I was fairly certain she was planning to go to Miko's presentation, and didn't know why that upset me. I couldn't be jealous of Miko, could I? Could it be that all this talk lately about sexuality was somehow getting on my nerves, making me wonder how satisfied Hadley and I were with each other? It's true we weren't getting it on like bunnies anymore, but we hadn't yet drifted into a state of complete indifference. At least I hadn't. And maybe I needed to make sure that Hadley hadn't either.

The very serious graduate student in my first workshop talked about the research Edward Donnerstein and others had been doing, most of it based on the response of male college students to pornography of different sorts. It went more or less like this: College-age males were exposed to pictures or films of varying degrees of sexual or violent behavior. Soft-focus, pleasurable sexual incidents were juxtaposed next to hardcore violence. The students were then given the opportunity to aggress against a male or female accomplice of the experimenter by supposedly delivering an electric shock or an aversive blast of noise. What the studies showed, the grad student said cautiously, is that the harmful effect of violent pornography came primarily from the fact that women were depicted as finding sexual violence arousing. Other than that the studies were somewhat inconclusive. In fact, it sounded as if men would respond aggressively to non-sexually explicit material if it were violent, material that wasn't classed as pornography at all.

The graduate student ended her talk by turning off the lights and showing slides of photos from *Playboy* juxtaposed with those from popular male detective magazines, magazines that were sold in many convenience stores. As images of women gagged and bound flashed by, she quoted from a study by Park Dietz that said that seventy-five percent of detective magazine covers depicted domination and thirty-eight percent bondage.

I got out of there before the discussion began. I was more agitated than I'd bargained for when I'd set out so eagerly for the conference this morning. It was hard to get the images of the bound and gagged women out of my head. I went out of the building and walked for ten minutes around the campus. Then I found a deserted place and did fifty push-ups and a hundred sit-ups.

I was a little late for the next workshop, "Sexist Images of Women in the Media." To my relief it was more witty than angry, facilitated by a woman I knew slightly, Mona Harris, who had run a small independent cinema once and now taught media studies at the university. She asked each of us to go around the room and to tell the group one image, one ad, one TV commercial that we found particularly stupid, offensive or just plain sexist. At first it was difficult to think—the outrage of the seventies was gone and we'd pretty much gone back to being accustomed to seeing partially naked young women used to sell products. One

woman said it was the age of the models that really bothered her. Since she'd read that ten- and eleven-year-old
girls were being made up to look older, that's all she saw
now, and it infuriated her that children, not even teen-
agers, were in *Vogue* and *Cosmo*. Another woman told a
funny story of watching an innocuous program on robins
with her young son and suddenly realizing how gender
polarization was being inculcated on children's TV.

One of my pet peeves was a TV commercial for some
brand of pantyhose, where a man's voice talked about how
fascinating, exciting, unpredictable, etc., Tracy or Stacy
was, giving you the impression that she was to be admired
for her strength, charm and personality, while at the same
time he was lifting her up and throwing her over his
shoulder so you got a good view of her long, stockinged
legs.

"Ros Coward, an English critic, writes in her book,
Female Desire, that 'the female body is the place where this
society writes its sexual messages,'" said Mona. "Whether
we want to or not we're all looking at women, all the
time."

A couple of women, probably lesbians, chortled self-
consciously, and Mona smiled, but went on seriously,
"Coward makes the point that looking isn't a neutral activity in Western culture. It's an activity which men have con-
structed in order to express domination and subordination.
The way women's bodies are portrayed over and over in
the mass media is sexualized, not just in a way that shows
the possibility of violence against them, but almost more
insidiously, in a way that shows their lack of economic and
social status relative to men."

Someone spoke up, "But studies show that porn *causes*
rape and sexual abuse. Sexist imagery might be unpleasant,
but it doesn't *hurt* anybody."

"I don't agree," said Mona. "The constant bombard-
ment of images that show women as subordinate does
more real damage to our sense of ourselves as women than
hardcore pornography, which is actually seen by a relative-

25

ly small part of the population."

"It doesn't matter what *women* look at," someone else said firmly. "It's what men look at that's important. And if they look at women being raped and enjoying it in pornography, that's what they'll act out."

"I think it *is* important what messages women take in," Mona argued. "And I see the reduction of the complexity of looking to the causal anti-porn theory that 'porn leads to violence and so it equals violence against women' as simplistic and ultimately harmful."

Mona stopped and looked at the clock, "We've run over, I'm sorry."

But someone had one more question: "So would you advocate censorship of any material?"

"Censorship of the kind Dworkin and MacKinnon advocate arbitrarily divides imagery into 'bad' and 'not so bad' material. Their call for censorship doesn't deal with important questions of how imagery is produced and for what reason. It doesn't come close to analyzing how the female body is used in this culture. All they're saying is that certain kinds of portrayals of sex and violence shouldn't be allowed."

I left the room enlightened, but still somewhat disturbed. Why did everybody have to talk about rape all the time?

It was lunch time and I went looking for Hadley. Outside one of the rooms in the corridor there was a knot of women, half in, half out of the door, and the noise of raised voices inside. I stopped to ask what was going on.

"It's Miko's workshop," someone said. "It started out with Miko talking about the historical repression of sexuality and the danger of the puritanical wing of the feminist movement trying to stop women from exploring what their sexuality really was. Then she showed two short videos— the first one something from your typical peepshow, with two lesbians making love sort of as a preliminary to the man coming in and giving them what they really wanted. Then Miko showed one of her own videos, which was a lot of revolting-looking close-ups of women's genitals and their hairy legs. And she asked what the difference was.

"Some women shouted that there was no difference, that both were products of the pornographic imagination, which essentially objectifies women and separates their sexuality from their personalities. And other women thought there was a difference—that Miko was showing women the way they really were and not all prettied up for the camera. They thought that Miko's video would actually turn off most male viewers. It turned off a lot of women anyway."

"Is that what they're still arguing about?" I asked.

"No, it's taken a new turn. It started when Miko was talking about being an *erotic dissident* and this contingent of women took over and said Miko wasn't really, that she still was representing established notions of sex, that it was just the same old vanilla sex as always. That they were the real sexual outlaws, because they were pushing the boundaries back."

"They're the S/Mers," someone else said. "One of them's even wearing a dog collar with a leash attached."

"This I have to see," I said, and squeezed into the room.

Nicky Kay, the woman I'd seen at the Espressomat the other day, was standing up in front of the roomful of women and talking. I hardly recognized her. Gone were the Oxford shirt, jeans and glasses. She was wearing a silky sort of see-through dress with black lacey underwear and a garter belt holding up sheer black stockings. Her eyes were heavily made-up and she had a hectic flush to her cheeks, and around her neck was a dog collar, black leather studded with silver spikes, the leash dangling over one shoulder. Next to her stood Oak, in black leather pants and a leather vest with no shirt underneath, wearing heavy black boots. On her wrists were wide leather bracelets with studs.

"Most of you know nothing about S/M and yet you condemn it," Nicky was saying. "What is it you're so afraid of? The lesbians here talk about being a minority sexual community and yet they refuse to allow us to have a forum to speak. Christians Against Pornography is invited to speak on a panel—not even about sexuality, but about pornography—but we're not invited. Why are we so threatening? I'll bet most of you haven't even thought about it. You take your cues from the rest of society, which is repressive and puritanical. You take your cues from the wave of the feminist movement that says sex is something that men do to us, that women don't like. Even the lesbians here are ashamed of female desire—or their lack of it. A lot of lesbians became lesbians for political reasons, not because of being attracted to women. It's that wing of the feminist movement that doesn't want us to speak our desires, that wants to silence us!"

"S/M isn't about sexuality, that's why!" someone shouted back at Nicky. "It's about degradation and patriarchal power and woman-hating!"

I saw Hadley over in a corner of the room and tried to move in her direction.

"S/M is about power, that's true, but it's about the flow of power. Power in heterosexual relations is frozen and static, with one side always dominant and one side always submissive. S/M is about movement and the exchange of energy."

Oak took up her line smoothly. "Unlike in the so-called real world, nothing in S/M is ever done without the consent of both people. That makes things a lot clearer and cleaner. There's a lot less of the emotional bullshit and power games between S/M dykes than between vanilla dykes."

"Sex between most lesbians isn't mutual," affirmed Nicky. "It's just a trade-off, first me, then you. But in S/M the possibility exists of opening all the way up, breaking limits you thought you had, satisfying yourself and your partner with incredible erotic intensity."

In spite of myself I was listening hard. That part sounded great. But...

"Why don't you talk about the pain and humiliation, Nicky?" A woman said. "About women with scars from razor blades all over their breasts, about women who've had internal hemorrhaging from being fist-fucked. About women who have to eat shit and drink urine. Don't just talk about power and trust; talk about broken arms and whip marks and burns from hot wax."

"S/M is about safety," Nicky said, two hot stains of red in her cheeks. "And you ought to know—you did it for years!"

Shock and scandal. The speaker was a well-known lesbian therapist.

I was still trying to get to Hadley. Over in the corner of the room I could see her familiar silver-blond head and straight nose.

"That's why I know about S/M from the inside," said the therapist bravely. "I know what a lie it is, and how it perpetuates the idea that degradation is acceptable and even good. Some women who've been sexually abused get into it as a way of trying to work through old feelings and to conquer them. I know, I was one. But it doesn't work, it's never going to work."

The room was buzzing. It was strange that Miko seemed to have retreated and was letting Nicky just take over like this. Maybe she was filming it from somewhere.

"Oh Christ, let's not be so melodramatic and hypocritical," said Nicky. "I bet three-quarters of you in this room have had rape fantasies, or fantasies of being tied up or forcing someone against her will. Let's be honest for once, okay, and not put it all on us. We're simply the most outspoken, but I bet most of you here have turned yourself on to some kind of S/M fantasies at one time or another."

Did she want a show of hands? She wasn't going to get it in this charged atmosphere. Instead, people seemed to be giving credence to Nicky's charge of hypocrisy and to be avoiding each other's eyes and trying to sneak out the door.

I moved to the back of the room through the gaps, and finally got close to where Hadley was. And Miko. Now it was obvious why Miko hadn't been participating in the discussion. She was whispering in Hadley's ear, and her hand was on Hadley's thigh.

4

Well, maybe not actually her *thigh*. In fact, afterwards I realized Miko was only tapping Hadley's leg slightly above the kneecap in order to make a point. But at the time—and in that sexually-charged atmosphere—I found any contact at all between them extremely upsetting, and I bolted from the room without listening to the end of the discussion. Something I also realized in retrospect was that, if I'd stayed, I might have made some connections I couldn't make until much later.

I decided to skip lunch, but as I was wandering forlornly around the campus I ran into Elizabeth Ketteridge, who offered me some trail mix. There was something unusual about her I thought; then I abruptly noticed she was pregnant. The weight had settled low on her, so that, with her smallish head and big eyes, she looked a little like a Russian doll.

"Isn't this an amazing conference, Pam?" she said as I took another handful of nuts and raisins. "I'm so glad it's happening. I think it's a real boost for the movement to have Loie Marsh here talking. After you've been in the movement so long you tend to get a little jaded." She paused a moment and added, "Not at *individuals'* stories, of course, but at the frequency and predictability of violence as a whole."

"Yes," I said. "I'm sure that's true." I didn't have to ask, what movement? Elizabeth belonged to a small but determined core of women in Seattle who had started the rape crisis center and who had managed to stick with it year after year.

"Is this your first?" I changed the subject.

"Oh no, my third," she said. "And my lover's been pregnant twice too. This will be our fifth."

"That's a lot of kids," I said weakly.

"We both come from big families—we love them." She smiled and patted my arm. "Good to see you, Pam," she said, and moved off.

I didn't understand it, this maternal urge. I was having trouble just being an aunt.

In the afternoon I decided to go to Loie Marsh's second workshop to see what all the fuss was about. Over the years I'd heard so many things—that she was charismatic, fanatic, misunderstood, paranoid, brilliant and obsessive. One thing she wasn't though, and that was boring.

The classroom was full, though not as full as Miko's had been. Maybe thirty women. Unlike some of the workshop leaders, who'd carefully arranged the chairs in a circle and taken their places among us, Loie left the chairs dutifully facing the blackboard and stood up in front of us like the commander of an insurgent army.

She managed to do it partly because she was a big woman, the kind whose ancestors had probably plowed the land in Norway and in North Dakota when they immigrated. Her shoulders were broad underneath the bright blue tunic she wore; her hands capacious. I noticed again that strangely bare, convex face, and the way not a strand of her short, curly blond hair touched her cheeks or forehead. Her eyes were a little small, but they missed nothing as we filed into the room, singly and in groups.

She was setting the tone already; she was the teacher, we the schoolgirls.

"Some of you," she began, when we were all assembled and were quiet, "may have gone, before lunch, to the workshop on lesbian pornography. Did anyone here go?"

Some women looked down at their feet. A couple of women raised their hands. Others stared at them.

"That workshop," said Loie, "and the discussion I've heard that came after it, is a perfect example of what I'm here to talk about today. The history of the anti-porn movement and the rise of the pro-dominance and submission element which threatens the very existence of feminism."

When Loie first began to speak, I was skeptical. People had said she was rhetorical. She was very rhetorical. Her speech patterns were those of a seasoned orator. Her words thundered, they whispered. She repeated herself; she arranged ideas in triads or in groups of triads, so they formed a rhythmic chant; she started out loud and then sank almost to silence; she started out soft and built to crescendos. She asked questions, she supplied answers.

What did she say? Afterwards I hardly remembered. All I know is at the time I was terribly moved by her sincerity, her dignity, her absolute compassion for any women who'd ever been used, abused or hurt by pornography. I was fully convinced that there was a conspiracy of sex-crazed lesbian deviants determined to endanger the serious efforts that women like Loie had spent years making on the behalf of women who had been victimized. Why did this conspiracy exist? So that these deviants could satisfy their male-identified lust. And further, because they thought that freedom meant having the same opportunity to objectify and degrade women, just as men had done for all recorded time.

At the very end there was a brief question and answer period. Most women wanted to know what they could do against the creeping threat of sexual liberalism in their community, but one woman timidly spoke up about something that obviously disturbed her deeply.

"Ummm. The thing is," she said. "I mean, the sexual liberals, they ah, well... What I'm wondering is, if you have fantasies... I mean, if you can't *help* having fantasies sometimes... I mean, what do you do with them?"

Loie gave her a piercing, yet kindly look. "I used to have fantasies," she said. "I regularly had fantasies of being raped, degraded and humiliated. That didn't mean I *wanted* any of those things to happen—in fact, when I *was* humiliated and degraded in real life, I *hated* it, and fought against it. What those fantasies meant, was that I had *internalized* male hatred. And once I realized that and didn't think those fantasies had anything to do with *me*, but with what Sheila Jeffreys has called the 'erotization of subordination' that is almost impossible to avoid in this country, if you're a woman, then those fantasies left me. *I stopped having fantasies.* I stopped having fantasies."

"Oh," said the woman. "Oh."

There was a fifteen-minute break between Loie's workshop and the next one I was planning to attend. I walked down the corridor and into the bathroom. I looked at myself rather grimly in the mirror. "It's good for you to be here," I said aloud. "Who cares about Miko anyway?"

When I came out of the bathroom I heard raised voices down the corridor, apparently coming from the room I'd just left. I tiptoed towards them. One of the voices was clearly Loie's: "I have a right to speak, nobody is going to stop me. I'll put it in my book, I'll tell whoever I want to. Don't you see, it will *help* the movement."

The other woman's voice was lower, almost threatening, and I strained to hear. Was it familiar? "Well, if you do, you'd better be prepared for... " She broke off. Had she heard my footsteps? The door to the room closed quietly.

Damn. Now that had sounded interesting.

*

I set off, somewhat reluctantly, to the workshop given by my friend Janis Glover the lawyer. She made a fairly lengthy presentation on the Minneapolis Ordinance that had been drafted by Andrea Dworkin and Catherine MacKinnon and vetoed by the mayor, but that had become the standard for much of the antipornography legislation the government and local communities were contemplating.

After Loie's passion the legal approach was infinitely cooler and more judicious. At first I couldn't get into it at all. Much of what Loie had said was still ringing in my ears: "The Constitution was written by white male slaveholders." "The First Amendment has no meaning for women who cannot express themselves." But gradually I began to listen to Janis talking about the difficulties of applying the ordinance, or ones like it, to reality. Unlike previous legislation having to do with obscenity and pornography, this ordinance had tried to make it an infringement of women's civil liberties to create and distribute pornography.

"Although Dworkin and MacKinnon claim to be against censorship, the new civil laws, which would allow individuals to sue the makers, sellers, distributors or exhibitors of pornography, would have the same censoring effect as criminal laws against obscenity. Materials could be removed from bookstores and libraries by the courts, and bookstores and publishers and librarians might have to deal with endless suits from individuals."

I found myself thinking of the workshop on current research and wishing there was a better way to distinguish between the different forms of pornography. Violent pornography, for instance, should maybe have a completely different name—aggressography?

"What Dworkin and MacKinnon did that was very innovative, but potentially legally unsound, was to define pornography as sex discrimination. Complaints could be

35

filed in the same way that complaints are filed against employment discrimination. The courts then would have the final say on whether the materials submitted to it fit the definition of pornography; if yes, the courts would have the authority to award monetary damages and to issue an injunction preventing further distribution of the material."

"But that was the great thing about the Minneapolis Ordinance," someone argued. "It would have put the legislative power in the hands of feminists."

"Not necessarily," said Janis. "Although women would have the power to file suit, the courts would have the final say on whether the materials submitted to it fit the definition of pornography. I don't need to remind you that the courts aren't exactly filled with progressive feminists."

"But legislation is the only possibility of stopping porn. It's used against racism—you don't disagree with censorship of racist materials?"

"I'm not sure that censorship ever works," said Janis. "Or that you can equate racism with pornography. I suppose I have a well-based fear of legislation doing the work that education should do. The combination of ignorance about sexuality that's fostered in our school systems and the hysteria of the New Right over abortion, homosexuality and AIDS make me very dubious that a law like the one proposed in Minneapolis would work to most of our advantage. Perhaps the ordinance would have focused so much good attention on sexual violence against women that it would have been worth it. My own feelings are that in this case the harm outweighed the potential good."

After the last workshop the conference participants began to gather in Pigott Auditorium to hear the closing speeches. I hadn't reconnected with Hadley all day and didn't see her now. I found June and Penny sitting together and joined them. June was dressed in red overalls and a little red beret that looked fetching against her dark skin; Penny was without Antonia for once and appeared a little frayed around the edges.

"Where were you all day?" I asked them.

"Just got here. I was at the mailing and June was with her kids. But June persuaded me that I should hear Gracie London."

"She's related to you or something, isn't she?"

"She used to be married to my cousin, the one who's being a journalist down in Oakland now. She was the first white person to marry into our family, wasn't that a trip. That was during the civil rights days and everyone was pretty suspicious. Now they like her a lot, even though she and Tad got divorced. The funny thing is, her kids identify as black, so she's still the only white person in the family. The only lesbian too." June winked at me. "So far."

Hadley hadn't come in yet. Restlessly I got up and moved to the back of the auditorium where I could look for her.

One of the organizers came on stage and thanked everyone for coming and making the conference such a success. She made about thirty-five announcements, from asking that Karen From Childcare please return to the Childcare Room, to telling us about four or five upcoming events. Finally she introduced the first speaker.

"For many of us, Gracie London is a familiar figure in Seattle. She has been active since the mid-sixties in civil rights and feminist issues. She founded the first reproductive rights groups in Washington State, was a founding board member of Rape Relief and is currently active in the anti-apartheid struggle. In addition to being a full professor of sociology at the University of Washington, she is the author of two books—*Understanding Women's Sexuality* [applause] and *Thinking About Abortion* [applause and some boos], and she is currently at work on a third book with the working title, *Enough Already: Sexuality Is Not the Only Issue* [an equal mixture of laughter and hisses]. Gracie London."

A good-looking woman in her late forties walked up to

the podium. She had short salt and pepper hair and an up-beat, no-nonsense air. She looked more like a company president than a sociology professor.

"When I was first asked to take part in today's conference I declined. Like many of you, I'm sure, I have come to be more and more ambivalent about saying what I think about sexuality and pornography, indeed, of knowing what I think about sexuality and pornography. Twelve or thirteen years ago, when I published my book on female sexuality, the situation seemed a lot simpler to me. Women's sexuality had been repressed and misrepresented for centuries; once we understood that, we could take it in new directions, develop a sexuality that was for ourselves. At the close of the eighties, that no longer seems such an easy prescription. Our sexuality is still repressed and mis-represented; young girls and boys get virtually no information on contraception, abortion rights are under attack, and the feminist movement is polarized on this issue as on no other.

"What I've come to speak to you about is about why the issue of pornography has become *the* issue. Asking that question has become more important for me than simply stating a position on the subject. If I had been asked to do that, to debate the anti-censorship side of the pornography debate, I would not be here today. I simply could not stomach another rehash of the same tired old discussion, even with such an illustrious debater as Loie Marsh. In-stead I wish to put to you some questions and come up with some possible answers as to why the issues of pornography and violence against women have become so central."

No sign of Hadley, though from where I was standing I had a good view of the open door leading to the lobby. It was empty except for a lone monitor looking at her watch. Through the glass doors of the lobby a walkway was vis-ible, leading through trees to the rest of the campus. Under the trees I could just about make out two figures. The one who faced me was Nicky Kay, with a leather jacket covering most of her S/M costume. She was still wearing her dog collar and leash, though, and I shuddered a little to think what the passing Jesuits must be thinking about this conference. The person she was talking to could have been a man or woman wearing a trenchcoat and a cap.

Gracie was warming up to her speech, but it was almost too much effort to listen to it. Compared with Loie, Gracie was low-key and far too rational. Perhaps we'd gotten too used to the chest-thumping evangelism of our favorite feminist speakers, who could make us respond with our hearts, not our heads.

"To many women, male hatred of women seems the only way to account for the fact that pornography seems to be increasing, for the fact of more and more women coming forward with stories of incest in childhood and physical abuse in their relationships with men. The view that supports these facts is based on acceptance of a certain biological interpretation of history—that men have used the penis as a weapon against women to force them into subordination. Anything that contradicts those assumptions—from the election of a government leader like Margaret Thatcher to the vocal presence of lesbian sadomasochists—is simply dismissed as male-identified behavior. Lesbian batterers are male-identified, female executives are male-identified, women in positions of political power are male-identified, women who don't call themselves feminists are male-identified, and women who don't agree with the views of the anti-pornography group are male-identified.

"One might reasonably ask, given the long list of women who, though they were born female, grew up female and consider themselves female, are not female-identified, who *is* female-identified?

"The answer, quite simply, is that you may identify as female if you identify as a victim or if you identify with women who are victims."

Outside Nicky and the figure in the trenchcoat appeared to be deep in discussion, if not in argument. Probably he was a reporter, lurking around the fringes of the conference. Or maybe he was propositioning Nicky. I saw her put her hands up to the dog collar around her throat; it looked like she was removing it.

"Those of us who disagree with women like Loie Marsh are not Uncle Toms or traitors to our class. We simply disagree.

"We disagree with the premise that there is one root cause for the inequalities of power between women and men and that that cause is male hatred of and sexual violence towards women. We do not say that this culture is not full of hatred towards women's bodies and violence towards women—to do so would be absurd, when all around us we see evidence of such hatred and violence. But we do not believe that that is the root cause, only one of many factors in the social construction of male/female inequality. Pornography and rape do not explain why there is so little daycare available for boys and girls; they do not explain why women in this country earn between fifty-nine and sixty-three cents for every dollar earned by a man. Pornography and rape do not explain why black women earn less than white women or why women in other countries earn least of all, sometimes only pennies a day. Pornography and rape do not explain why so few women are the heads of profitable businesses or charitable organizations, why so few women are mayors, governors, congresspeople and presidents. They do not explain why there is war—if men hate women so much, why do they kill them individually on the streets rather than massacre them in the thousands as they do their fellow men during wartimes?"

I glanced through the doors again. Nicky and whomever she'd been speaking to were gone. Now Gracie began to come to her conclusion, but I felt almost indifferent. Gracie said what she thought, while Loie told us what to think. That was the difference: Gracie made mental demands, Loie made a heartfelt appeal. In my intellectual weariness I found myself longing for Loie to rise up, like a Biblical prophet, to tell us all what was wrong and what we should do.

"To believe that maleness is intrinsically evil is a deliberate strategy and, I think, quite arbitrary. Almost all of the anti-porn activists are white, yet they do not seem to believe that whiteness is intrinsically *evil*, even though, as far back as we know, people of lighter skin have tortured, murdered, exploited and patronized their darker brothers and sisters. A good many of the anti-porn activists are from middle- or upper-class homes, yet they do not seem to believe that it is intrinsically *evil* to have been born into social privilege, even though for all recorded history, the rich have killed, exploited and patronized the poor. Few of the anti-porn activists are disabled, but they do not make a point of telling us that it is intrinsically *evil* to have been born able-bodied, though there has never been a time when the disabled have been respected and cared for as contributing members of the society.

"The point is not which 'ism' is the root cause of oppression in our civilization, which sex or class or race is the most oppressed. The point is about the social construct of power. Those who have power will never willingly give it up—whether that power is based on gender, wealth or white skin. For power is never or rarely given up—it is seized. Not by people who are passive victims, but by people whose oppression empowers them to act and, I submit, by people who, when and if they manage to obtain power, will quite likely find the means to abuse it in very much the same ways."

5

THERE WAS A SILENCE after Gracie had finished and then, a series of diverse applauses, from thunderous in some quarters to subdued and thoughtful in others, splashing against each other like waves in a choppy sea. Some people seemed confused by the ambiguity of Gracie's ending note, and I heard a woman nearby say to her companion, "Is she saying women are as bad as men?" During the pause before Loie was introduced, a number of people came in and found seats down in front. I wondered if they were Loie-supporters who'd been boycotting Gracie's speech. Hadley was among them; I grudgingly caught her attention and we both slipped into the seats Penny and June had been saving for us. She raised her eyebrows several times to express what an exciting event this was, but I ignored her. I was pretty sure she'd been hanging out with Miko and didn't like that one bit.

"I'm sure this speaker needs no introduction," said the conference organizer, and then proceeded to give her a very long one. Naturally, for Seattlites, the most important fact was that Loie had been born in Seattle. That alone was worth all the articles published, the speeches given. The audience whooped at the word "native."

I had wondered what tactic Loie would adopt to counteract the generally favorable impression of down-to-earth skepticism that Gracie had just made. Would Loie be righteously angry or coldly negating? She was neither. She was simply sad.

"Sisters," she began, and her tone was infinitely weary and yet warm. "I wish I could tell you how much of what I have heard and seen here at this conference today has disheartened and distressed me. There was a time once—years ago now—some of you may not even remember it—when to say you were a feminist was something to proud of. You knew what it meant. It meant standing up and speaking out against the things that hurt you and hurt other women. It meant being laughed at and jeered and dismissed by men. But not caring. Because you knew what you were up against. You knew what the odds were and that they were stacked against you. They had been stacked against you for centuries. Yet this time you believed that you—with the help of hundreds of thousands of other women—that this time, at this precise historical moment—you would manage to change the world."

Loie's voice had been gradually building up, but now it sank again, despondent and almost wistful. In spite of myself I felt drawn into the mood of it, hypnotized by the soft, almost elegiac quality of her voice.

"In those days—oh, it seems like a million years ago now, doesn't it?—it seemed so easy to talk about 'sisterhood.' We knew what sisterhood meant and we knew who our enemy was. Our enemy was the patriarchy, in all its various forms, the patriarchy that had dominated our lives for all those many thousands of years. In spite of what some women—the revisionist historians—now say, we never divorced issues of race and class from our analysis of women's oppression. How could we? After all, many of us had *come* from the civil rights and student or peace movements and it is *clear* that things are always worse for poor women and women of color. It's just that we found, and hundreds of women found, that traditional assumptions

43

about the nature of power were no longer *sufficient* to explain what we saw in our daily lives—which was *systematic* subordination of women's rights to the male desire for power and control."

Loie's voice dropped again and now the sadness was that of someone who has been very deeply betrayed. "Yes, in those days the world was a simpler place. We knew who our friends were, we knew who our enemies were. But increasingly it has become apparent that women who were once our friends are now our enemies. (Loie looked meaningfully in the direction of some leather-jacketed women down right.) They are women who have, instead of turning their backs on pornography, chosen to embrace it, to pretend that their degradation or their imposition of degradation on others is based on choice, on 'consent.' They have eroticized their subordination and called it 'freedom.' These women have allied themselves with male-identified heterosexual women leftists, with male civil libertarians and pornographers, and with gay men, to fight us on the very issues it once seemed we all agreed on.

"I don't deny that it hurts. It hurts politically—and it hurts personally—to have former colleagues, women you *thought* were feminists, turn against you and revile you in public. I'm sure that on many occasions a lot of us have thought of just giving up. It often seems just *too hard* to be attacked from both sides.

"So why don't I just give up? Why don't all of us just give up? We're never going to see the end of abuse against women in our lifetimes, so why not just give up now, why not call it a day and just say, I've done what I could but they were stronger, better funded, had better connections. Why not just accept that there has always been rape, pornography, prostitution and violence against women and be done with it? Why not just accept that every time, for the rest of our lives, when we go to a film, open a book or magazine, turn on the TV, that there is more often than not going to be some image or some incident that confirms male power over women, that confirms that women exist

44

to be used by men? Why not just accept that every time we go out on the street that we can be raped? That we can be humiliated and battered and raped in our homes and on our jobs? That our daughters and our daughters' daughters will grow up in the same way, afraid, terrified underneath, and that our sons and our grandsons will grow up knowing that they have the power to terrorize. . . .

"Well," and Loie paused and looked at us like a big Nordic goddess looking down on a pack of frail human beings, with a mixture of tenderness and resolve, "I'll tell you why I don't give up, and why many of us refuse to give up. It is because of women like Karen Ann Jones, once known as Dolly Delight, who lives with the knowledge that her forced degradation in dozens of films is still being shown everywhere in the world, making millions of dollars for the men who forced her into such degradation. It's because of all of us, and I'm including myself, friends and relatives, who were once in positions that we imagined were freely chosen, but in fact were forced upon us, positions where our humanity was degraded, where we were used to make messages that conveyed pleasure in degradation, where. . . "

Loie seemed to be looking down at someone in the audience, and then she abruptly broke off. For an instant she appeared confused, almost angry, then she recovered herself and quickly brought her speech to a close, with a trembling urgency that had some of the audience wildly clapping before she had even finished. What had Loie been about to say? And what had stopped her? I strained my neck to see who it was she'd noticed in the audience, but I was too far back.

"I work against pornography, in spite of enemies on the right and on the left because I can't do anything else. For my self-respect and for the self-respect of the millions of humiliated women who depend on me to speak for them. Thank you."

The applause was thunderous, and cries of "Loie, Loie" filled the air.

45

Penny nudged me. "You really think there are millions of humiliated women out there, with no one to speak for them but Loie?"

"Shhh!" said the woman behind us.

During the dinner break before the panel discussion was to begin, Penny, June, Hadley and I went to an Ethiopian restaurant nearby. It was packed with women from the conference. I saw Nicky and Oak and their S/M crowd come in. Nicky hung up her leather coat on the coat rack by the door. She was no longer wearing her dog collar, but looked highly excited.

We were lucky enough to get a table right away. Between sopping up the sauces with that spongy sour white bread they serve, we discussed the different styles of Gracie and Loie.

"The thing I hate," said June, "is that speakers like Loie who are doing the doom and gloom number on us always have to throw in phrases like, 'And for black women, the situation is even worse.' We're not a statistic to be tacked onto the general discussion. And besides, why is it worse? Abuse is abuse."

"It's because they can't deal with racism other than further victimization," Penny said. "So if things are bad for white women, who are supposed to be the norm, they must be *really* bad for black women."

"I liked what Gracie said," mused Hadley. "I've been asking myself why I haven't had a clear position on pornography, like I should have one, and not why this particular discussion has become so important all of a sudden."

I didn't know why, but I suddenly had the urge to defend Loie. "She's incredibly sincere, Loie. I had the feeling that she's been through a lot herself, that it's more than a political cause for her, that she really identifies with women who've been victimized."

"Do you think so?" June was skeptical. "I think she's

46

just got a big mouth and she likes to hear herself talk. She'd be nobody if there was a really was an end to pornography."

"That woman Miko has a bigger mouth," said Penny. "The panel tonight should be interesting. I heard that her workshop today practically turned into a riot. Did either of you go?"

"Uh, well. . . " Hadley mumbled, avoiding my eyes. "I stopped in."

"I went," I said. "I was surprised actually at how little Miko had to say. To the workshop anyway."

"Oh," said Hadley.

When we got back to the auditorium just before seven-thirty it was packed. A slightly different crowd was here now; in addition to many of the straight and lesbian feminists there were men, the sort in beards and flannel shirts and the sort in suits. There were also more working women in heels and jackets.

Events like this never started on time, so I didn't think anything of it when seven-forty-five came and went with no panelists appearing at the long table covered with pitchers of water and microphones. The four of us talked, though actually Hadley and I didn't talk too much to each other. We weren't having a Fight; we were having a Little Distance.

But as it neared eight o'clock and there was still no sign of anyone on the stage, the audience began to get restless. People stood up and walked around, started conversations with strangers or with friends across the aisles. I saw a lot of familiar faces. Nicky and Oak, who had still been finishing their dinner when we left the restaurant, came in and joined a small crowd of leather dykes down in the front row. I wondered if they were planning to heckle Loie. I saw Hanna Sandbakker with a tall, white-haired man. I wondered if it was her father, Loie's uncle. They also came in a bit late and had to stand in back. Standing near the stairs that led up to the stage were the panelists: Elizabeth, serenely pregnant, chatting with various people; Miko, in a black jumpsuit and a red turban, vibrating with energy; Gracie looking a little tired, as if she wanted it all to be over.

Finally one of the conference organizers, looking worried and apologetic, came out on stage. "We'll be starting in just a minute," she said. "Thank you all for your patience. We've been waiting for Loie Marsh, but unfortunately she seems to have been delayed. So we'll just begin without her and hope that she joins us soon."

The panelists went up on stage and took their places at a long table. The three I knew were joined by Sonya Gustafson. I'd never seen her before and had been expecting a mousy-looking woman wearing a flower print dress, but she strode after Elizabeth, as poised and as striking as any of them, in a linen pantsuit, expensive scarf and gold earrings.

Gracie started things off by giving a capsule version of her speech earlier that afternoon. She seemed more subdued, but still very cogent as she asserted that antipornography activists had gotten off on the wrong track.

Sonya Gustafson was next. In a calm, authoritative voice she talked about child pornography rings and the things done to children in the name of porn.

"Many liberal and otherwise decent people like to pretend that pornography is created by consenting adults for consenting adults. Since relatively few of us ever consume hardcore pornography, we may assume that it hasn't changed much from the days when *Playboy* first appeared, or that the issue is one of free speech, reminiscent of the era when books like *Ulysses* were banned from sale in this country. If you do assume that pornography is relatively harmless and that the issue is one of puritanism opposed to more liberal sexual values, I urge you to take a trip to one of the stores downtown and to take a look at what really is for sale. I think you will be as shocked as I was. In addition to the usual fare of bondage, domination and violence, you will find pictures that are guaranteed to turn your stomach: photographs of small children, four and five years old, mounted by huge men, very tiny children forced to have intercourse, and yes, even babies, girls and boys, with their genitalia exposed and vulnerable to penetration."

Sonya went on relentlessly with descriptions that did indeed turn many of our stomachs. She didn't mention the fundamentalist belief system that underlay her arguments against porn, she didn't bring up some of the other goals of the moral majority to which she belonged, like putting homosexuals in concentration camps to prevent them from spreading AIDS and making abortion and contraception illegal. Sonya only talked about pornography's abuse of children, and when she got to her stories of the little blond Minnesota girl who was kidnaped off her playground and sold in Los Angeles for use in porn films, there wasn't a mother or a father in the house who felt easy in their seats. Penny, beside me, was completely agitated. "I never knew any of this. I never knew any of this."

Elizabeth, if anything, was even more persuasive. Not only was she cute and pregnant, but she gave off the aura of vast experience, which indeed she did have. She talked primarily about the contract work she'd done with sex offenders, both sexually abusive fathers and other relatives, and rapists.

"Most of the offenders I worked with were exposed to or involved with pornography at a very early age. They tended to have an obsessive relationship with porn. Sometimes their families have found stacks of magazines in their closets, their basements, their garages. It's taken over their lives, it's become their entertainment, their way of life. Let me tell you the results of some studies we made. In psychological testing most of our offenders seem predisposed to violent acting-out behavior. Many of them state that they think pornography is directly responsible for where they got their ideas about women and about what sexuality is. Many of them say that the exposure to pornography early in their lives had a direct effect on them and contributed strongly to their need to act out."

My stomach was churning and tense, but I had to keep listening.

"Let me talk a little about adults who sexually abuse children. A recent study reports that one of the major reasons why children don't report being sexually abused is that the abusers convince them that such activity is normal and pleasurable. They routinely use pictures of child pornography to convince the children of how enjoyable it is. . . . "

I could see that I wasn't the only one who felt sick hearing this. In any audience full of women it's probable that at least one out of four will have been sexually violated in some way. At some point in Elizabeth's careful recounting of statistics I realized I couldn't listen any more and just shut down. As far as I was concerned, everything she said made sense and was true and horrible and frightening. And I didn't want to hear it.

So much of the effect of a panel discussion lies in the order of the speakers. Miko, coming after Sonya and Elizabeth, was hard put to equal their quiet, passionate power. Starting off on the wrong foot by announcing that she too had once been afraid of and threatened by pornography, but that now she saw it as the way to her personal salvation, Miko went on to tell the audience many particulars of her sexual and creative life. But her nervousness made her appear off-key and strident instead of being a woman powerfully in touch with her eroticism. It wasn't just my prejudice either. Miko, who so loved a public forum for her cultivated outrageousness, was definitely not in tune with the atmosphere tonight as she told story after embarrassing story of what her life had been like before and after she discovered the liberating power of making videos of women's body parts.

"Who cares?" I heard June sigh, but when I snuck a glance at Hadley, she looked fascinated.

The discussion with the audience began with Miko and Gracie bearing the brunt of the attacks. One woman wanted to know how Miko could justify promoting pornography when innocent children were being abducted right and left. Someone from Radical Women called Miko decadent and then went on to say that Gracie hadn't gone nearly far enough with her analysis of the capitalist and imperialist origins of patriarchy. Gracie managed to respond to her with civility and dispatch, but she didn't stand a chance against a nasal young woman who wanted to talk about Julia Kristeva's theories of female language. It was only when some of the audience began to protest that the speaker stopped droning on.

The protests started at the back of the audience and moved forward like the tide. It was only when the murmuring reached our row that I realized it wasn't about Julia Kristeva at all.

"Something happened to Loie Marsh. . . . " The tide broke over us and flowed on.

"What?"

"Loie—someone found her."

"Who?"

"Loie. Marsh. She was. . . "

"Dog collar."

"What?"

"They said she was strangled."

"Loie Marsh was strangled by a dog collar."

"Oh my god."

The tide of rumor reached the stage, but couldn't climb it. The panelists looked out, bewildered, at the sea of talk. For an eerie second or two there was a silence. Then someone screamed, very loudly, "You've all killed her."

In the distance you could just hear the police sirens approaching.

6

THERE WERE TWO TYPES of Monday mornings at Best Printing. The kind where everyone came in at exactly a quarter to nine, primed on caffeine or good spirits and ready to get down to work immediately, and the kind of morning we were having the Monday after the conference on sexuality.

June lolled on one end of the long sofa reading the newspaper and groaning softly. Ray sat on the other end, coaxing Antonia with a pacifier, an adoring, absent look on his face. Penny sat, most unlike herself, in a slumped position over her desk, trying to focus on a cup of coffee. Something about her strongly reminded me of our mother, maybe the way the oversize glasses sat on her small, sharp nose; maybe the way her dry, half curly hair stuck out. Once her short brown hair had been kept artificially perpendicular with mousse, now it had an indifferent perm and was parted on the side. Penny the svelte had gotten careless about her dress too and seemed to go about in stained sweatshirts that she could whip up at the sound of a cry.

She was definitely slowing down. The first week after having Antonia she'd been, if possible, even more efficient than before. She always seemed to have the baby in one arm, a satchel in the other and her car keys out and jingling.

June had said, "She'll get over it. She's just trying to prove that, unlike most women, having a baby has not changed her in the slightest."

Now she leaned her head on the desk and tried to get the coffee into her mouth without lifting the cup.

Even Moe was uncharacteristically dreamy and stood by the big window looking out at the blue September sky. I wondered if he was thinking about Allen or about the life he'd left in San Francisco. The two of them had moved up to Seattle in July after two of their best friends had died the same week. Moe had been exhausted with grief, but for Allen it was worse. "He's got survivor's guilt," Moe had said, "Except he can't believe he's really a survivor." Allen had turned into a nervous hypochondriac, calling the doctor once or twice a week and constantly checking his body for signs of disease.

A neat quick man in his thirties, with lots of soft dark curls and blue eyes, Moe was a gem to have around the shop. He was the best cameraman and designer we'd ever had; he was far too good to be working at Best, he could have, and he had had, a very good union job. But he wanted to be out, he needed to be out at work, he said. Now more than ever.

"Well, it doesn't look good for Seattle," said June gloomily from the sofa, throwing down the paper. "Nobody appreciates you while you're here, so you go away to get famous, you come back and they kill you."

"Hanna must be in shock," said Ray. "Have you tried to call her, Penny?"

Penny rolled her head on the desk: No.

"We could go over there later," Ray suggested. "She might like some support."

I was thinking aloud: "But why then? Why was Loie killed *then*, between her closing speech and the evening panel? And why was she strangled with a dog collar? Of all the offensive weapons to use, that had to be the absolute *most* offensive to someone like Loie."

"I don't understand," said Ray.

Moe and I looked at each other. "You tell him, dear," I said.

"The dog collar wasn't made for a *dog*, Ray," Moe explained. "I mean, it wasn't just someone who was out walking their dog and decided to put Loie on a leash instead. Dog collars are used by sadists on masochists to denote ownership and dominance in the S/M ritual. And since Loie was one of the most prominent opponents of S/M, it seems like it may have been an attempt to discredit her."

"Poor Loie," Penny said, "to have fought so hard against pornography, and then to die like that."

"Unless," I said slowly. "You don't think... No, not Loie... But wouldn't that be a scandal!"

Penny called up Hanna eventually and, over her protestations, went to see her with Ray and Antonia that afternoon. She came back alone; Ray had taken Antonia to the doctor for a check-up.

"The cops had just left when I got there. They'd been asking Hanna questions all morning and then they'd gone through Loie's things. It's all been really terrible for Hanna. I mean, she hadn't seen Loie since Loie went off to Boston, not for *years*, then a couple of weeks ago Loie calls up and says she's coming to Seattle. She's broken up with her girlfriend and needs to get away and a quiet place to work on her book—what could Hanna say? They're cousins after all, they were practically brought up together. So Loie turns up with all this stuff, boxes of notes and newspaper clippings, and just moves in. It's all been really upsetting for Hanna, and I'm sure it's going to be upsetting for everyone. How are they going to find the person who killed Loie? What do the police know about the anti-porn movement or about lesbian sadomasochists?"

"Well, we don't know for sure it was anyone from the S/M community," I said. "It could just as easily have been someone who didn't like Loie personally and just decided to play a very cruel joke on her."

Penny looked at me with some interest. "Are you going to follow this up, Pam?"

"Me?"

"Why not? We know for sure the police are going to make a botch-up of the whole thing. Think about Hanna. They'll probably suspect *her*—in fact, I'm sure they suspect her already."

"I wouldn't even know where to start."

"Start with the dog collar."

After work I went up to Capitol Hill to meet Hadley. The Espressomat, quite naturally, was fizzing with the murder, and gossip being the expansive gas that it is, all sorts of details had been added and elaborated on. Some people were saying that Loie had been found handcuffed, bound and gagged; others said that she was a hypocrite, that "everyone knew" she was into S/M.

It was all pretty revolting. It wasn't that I'd been particularly drawn to Loie, but I'd believed—and I still believed—that she had a lot of integrity. She might have had secrets, even sexual secrets, but I didn't think the practice of sadomasochism was one of them.

Start with the dog collar, Penny had said. Well, it wouldn't hurt to do a *little* checking around. Where did you buy those things, anyway? Since it appeared that Hadley was going to be here for a while longer, I decided to go down the street to the alternative General Store.

I couldn't bring myself to ask for what I wanted at the main counter, so I went back to the hardware section and cornered Abby, a friend of mine who worked there.

"Abby, hi," I whispered. "Do you have any dog collars?"

"I didn't know you had a dog, Pam. Or are you getting

a dog, what kind of dog?"

"No, I don't have a dog," I said, still trying to convey by my whisper that we should keep our voices down. "I'm, uh, not looking for *that kind* of dog collar."

"Ohhhh," she said appraisingly. "Sex life starting to drag a little? You'd be very surprised how many people come in here looking for stuff like that. Yeah, the other day a guy came in here and asked if we had chain link. I told him where the roll was—when I came around the corner to see how he was doing, darned if he wasn't down on his knees with a length of it around his neck. He said he was measuring it for his dog."

"Abby," I whispered furiously. "Would you lower your voice a little, please? This isn't what you think. I'm just interested—because of Loie. It has nothing to do with my sex life."

"Well, you won't find what you're looking for here. Just little blue puppy dog and kitty cat collars here. And lots of flea collars. Tell you where to go though. The Vault."

"The Vault?"

"It's not far away. It's a sex shop—mainly gay male, but lots of leather, B & D stuff too."

"B & D?"

"Bondage and Domination."

"Oh." Why didn't she feel embarrassed saying words like that aloud? I did. "Well, thanks, Abby."

"Sure Pam." She called after me, "I didn't *think* you'd suddenly got a *dog*."

I went back to the Espressomat. Hadley was still in the thick of it.

"I'm sorry," she said. "Lynda had to leave early today for an appointment with her iridiologist and the place is packed. Probably because of the conference and Loie. If you want to go on home, I promise I'll be there by seven-thirty. Morgan is starting her shift at seven."

"Okay," I said. "I'll make some dinner."

I didn't go straight home though. I decided to stop by The Vault.

It was a seedy looking place and I couldn't help scouting the street before I ducked inside. Once in it took me a minute to accustom myself to the layout. I wasn't sure where to look. At the front were innocent love orgy oils and skimpy underwear. At the back were racks of videos and magazines. But I headed first to a side wall festooned with a lot of black leather. Before I got there, however, my attention was arrested by four or five shelves of vibrators and dildos. It was like a forest of off-pink flesh, with occasional black trees and roots.

Astounded, I stopped and looked more closely. Some of these things were huge, three feet long, five inches thick, some of them with two heads. How—and where—did people fit them into such orifices as they possessed? I was more amazed than judgmental when I turned away to face the wall. Off it hung black leather caps, vests, pants with buttocks or crotches cut out, gloves. The only thing that was missing was black leather socks.

I wasn't sure exactly what to make of it. Why was it all leather, why was it black? All it reminded me of when I looked at it was Nazi Germany—I wondered if it was supposed to. Inside the glass cases in front of the wall were smaller objects, all labeled. Butt plugs, hand and leg cuffs, tubes to encase the penis, cock rings and nipple clamps. Ouch! On top of the cases were more of the things I'd been looking for: whips of different lengths and strands, leashes, studded jock straps and, aha, dog collars. Big thick ones with spikes, like the kind Nicky Kay had worn, like the kind I presumed had strangled Loie.

A man with a pleasant smile came over and asked if he could help me find anything.

I blushed beet-red, and squeezed out, in a tiny voice, "Oh no, just looking." But before he moved off, I managed to ask more firmly if I could possibly try on one of the dog collars.

I glanced around before I slipped it on my neck, to make sure no one I knew was in the store. No, just some men perusing the magazines.

"Now you don't want it too tight," the man cautioned.

But that was just what I did want. I tried pulling one end of the collar through the buckle. As the clerk looked on in bemusement I felt my eyes popping a little and my breath being choked off. Still, you'd have to be pretty strong to choke someone who was struggling. The end of the collar was quite short for trying to pull it. And Loie was a big woman. If she weren't cooperating it would be hard to get her to stand still to pull the end of the collar, much less to slip it around her neck in the first place.

And if she were cooperating? I shook the idea out of my head.

"Is it working for you?" the man asked sympathetically.

I hastily pulled the collar off, and said I didn't think so, that I'd just look around a little more.

I investigated the videos first and then the magazines. I'd never been in a store like this one before, and after I got over my initial timidity and shock, was more curious than offended. The main thing that had struck me so far was how incredibly expensive everything was. No wonder the porn industry turned over eight billion dollars a year when they charged ten or fifteen dollars for a magazine and asked a sixty dollar deposit to rent a video. But as I looked further I began to feel other sensations.

I remembered something Mona had said during her workshop Saturday on sexist images. "All the anti-porn movement is protesting is nudity and violence and all they want to do is remove the images of women that are most offensive and blatant. Most of us go along with that, accepting their word for it. But how many of us have ever really taken a good look at what's available in the pornography marketplace? How do we *know* that most of what's sold as pornography is really more offensive than a typical issue of *Cosmopolitan* or an episode of *Dynasty*?"

I guessed this was my chance to find out.

Some of the pictures turned me on, I couldn't deny it. All that lust, everywhere I looked: men doing things to men, women doing things to men, men doing things to women, women doing things to women, everybody with large primary and secondary sexual characteristics and everybody with their eyes bulging out in carnal delight. Still, after a bit, it palled. As Abby had said, there *was* a lot of bondage and domination. It wasn't just women being dominated by men however; there were lots of pictures of dominatrixes (in black leather of course) grinding a sharp stiletto heel in some poor slob's back.

After about thirty minutes my curiosity had turned from lust to queasiness to a sad feeling that human beings had been created for another purpose than to loll around with their tongues sticking out, having their various orifices and protruberances photographed and sold for great sums of money. I didn't know what that purpose was—I didn't think we had been created to participate in television game shows either—but it had to be different from this.

I was just replacing a magazine called *Lesbian Enema Lust* on the rack when I heard a familiar voice behind me.

"Well, Pam, I never expected to find *you* in a place like this."

It was Miko, wearing a short leather jacket, skin tight purple stretch pants and tall, embossed boots.

I was so taken aback that *Lesbian Enema Lust* fell from my hand. Miko picked it up.

"Wow," she said. "I've never seen this one before. Does Hadley know you're here?"

"Leave Hadley out of this." My voice had returned. "It's my own business what I'm doing here. And another thing, I'm sick of you chasing after Hadley."

Miko seemed flabbergasted in her turn. "Me—running after Hadley? You must be imagining things. She's not my type and even if she was, it's clear the two of you are a couple. I may not be into monogamy, but I'm not into triangles."

"Well, then why are you always flirting with her? And asking her to come see your sex videos?"

"Oh, I do that with everyone," Miko laughed. "It's just how I am. It's PR. Remember, I invited you too."

I didn't know whether to let myself be mollified. Maybe she was just trying to throw me off the track.

"Well, what are *you* doing here?" I asked her.

"Me? I come here all the time. Sometimes I rent a video, or see what the new magazines are. I buy my copies of *On Our Backs* and *Bad Attitude* here. Do you ever read them?"

"What are they?"

"Lesbian sex magazines. They're a lot of fun. The photography could be slicker, but what can you do? It's low budget. The articles are interesting. . . . Isn't that what men used to say about *Playboy*? 'I read it for the articles.'"

Miko flipped open a copy for me to see. Two very attractive young white women, bare-bosomed and in lace petticoats, were gently touching each other. It didn't seem so bad. Then I noticed that each of them had one nipple pierced with a ring linked to a chain that the other was pulling. The petticoats were lightly spotted with blood.

I closed the magazine and handed it back to Miko. "This isn't my kind of thing."

Miko tucked it under her arm and sighed, "I can't help it, Pam. I like you. You're such a straight little arrow. Though I still can't imagine what you're doing in here. Unless it has something to do with Loie's death. Somebody told me that's a hobby of yours, investigation."

I didn't say anything.

"Well, if you're really looking into Loie's murder, you're not going to be able to avert your eyes from some pretty nasty stuff I imagine. So you might as well enjoy it!" Miko whirled provocatively and sauntered to the cash register.

7

THE NEXT AFTERNOON after work Hadley and I went downtown to the Fun Palace on First Ave to see if we could find Nicky Kay. Hadley wasn't too sure how much she wanted to get involved with this whole thing, but I persuaded her. I didn't particularly want to go alone and I had the feeling that if anyone knew anything about dog collars, it would be Nicky.

Even though Hadley was along I still felt uneasy going into the Fun Palace. Just as when I'd entered The Vault, I gave a hasty but thorough glance around to see if anyone I knew was watching.

We asked for Nicky and were told she was working. Dancing. "You'll need quarters if you plan on watching her."

I was taken aback. "Oh we didn't plan on *watching*... Can't we give her a message that we'd like to see her?"

"She don't get a break till seven and the boss don't like her to talk to customers on the premises."

No use arguing that we didn't think of ourselves as *customers* for godsakes. We bought five dollars' worth of quarters and made our way to the exotic dancing booths.

They were arranged in an L-shaped pattern, two corridors of doors each with a light above. Some were lit up red—they were occupied. There apparently were two kinds of booths: those with a one-way mirror and those with a two-way. We stood in the corridor debating in whispers which kind we should choose. There were more with one-way mirrors.

"How're we going to get a message to her if she can't see it?"

"We should make sure she's there first."

So we crowded into one of the one-way booths. It was a tight fit for two, dim and shabby, with shag carpeting on the floor and walls. Something under my feet felt wet and sticky—I tried not to think about it. On one wall was a small plastic screen with a coin receptacle under it; when we put in a quarter the screen went up slowly, revealing a brightly lit room. In front of a wall of mirrors three women were dancing naked to soft rock music.

"Whew," said Hadley.

All three of them were wearing high heels and one wore a wide belt. They danced well, if a little perfunctorily, in smooth gyrations. One of the women was Nicky. Again she looked different from the times I'd seen her before, but it wasn't just because she didn't have any clothes on. Her soft brown hair was gathered up on her head with a butterfly clamp; she was wearing a small forest of fake lashes and lots of black eyeliner; her armpits and legs were shaved and her fingernails were painted fire engine red.

"I've always wondered what my customers did when they left the Espressomat," Hadley joked, but her light tone changed when she saw the screen going down. "Quick—put another quarter in!"

The music had gotten slower, sexier. Nicky swayed into it and threw back her head, singing the bluesy lyrics. The other two women didn't seem quite as much into it. They were younger, a little vague about the eyes. One of them moved as if the lower half of her body didn't really belong to her. She went up to one of the windows and, still dancing, spread her legs and thrust her pelvis out casually.

Hadley put in two more quarters.

"I can't help it, Pam," she said. "This is turning me on. Is she going to do that to us?"

"Hadley, look at her eyes. Don't just look at her crotch. She's doing a job for money—she's probably thinking about something completely different, like whether she took the hamburger out to thaw for tonight's dinner."

I found Nicky far sexier. And I think it was partly because she was good at her job. which was to create the illusion that she was in a state of sexual heat, easy and uninhibited with her body, ready to satisfy and be satisfied. She really seemed to be enjoying herself, enjoying dancing and moving her limbs—not so much exposing herself as showing off. I wondered how it would feel to know that a dozen men (or women, perhaps, like us) were staring avidly at your naked body.

Hadley was putting more quarters in. I tried to stop her. "We've got to move to a two-way booth—so we can communicate with her."

"All right," Hadley agreed, unenthusiastic. "But it's going to be different. They'll know two women are watching them. And I bet they won't like it."

The dancer with the detached eyes and flexible pelvis had made her way over to our booth and was pressing her crotch up against our window like a sea anemone at an aquarium.

"Oh my god," said Hadley. "I can't decide whether it's horrible or it's wonderful."

"Come on, Hadley—didn't you ever do one of those women's self-help health groups? If it weren't for the music and the sinful atmosphere, it'd be just like doing a cervical check-up."

Our screen went down for the last time. We'd spent $2.50 in ten minutes. Out in the corridor a couple of men were waiting; they looked surprised and embarrassed when they saw us. One of them hastily ducked into the booth we'd left and the other stared at the floor. He was a middle-aged businessman in a suit.

"You'll like the girls," Hadley told him enthusiastically. "One of them's got a great pair of tits."

He turned and fled down the corridor.

After a few minutes a two-way booth opened up and we went in. We put all the rest of our quarters in the slot and our screen went up. One of the dancers gave us a casual glance and then looked again, her mouth tightening. Hadley smiled, to try to put her at her ease, but she turned away with an emotion we couldn't read, and moved over to another window.

"I knew they wouldn't like it," said Hadley. "She probably thinks we're perverts."

"Well?"

"Look—Nicky's looking our way. Hold up your sign."

I held it flat against the window. It said: NICKY COULD WE PLEASE SPEAK TO YOU DURING YOUR BREAK? IF YES MEET US AT THE FRANK-FURTER ON THE CORNER AT 7 P.M.

She stared at the sign, then at us. Without changing the tempo of her dancing she nodded her head slightly.

"I guess we have to go now?" said Hadley.

"We've gotten what we came for."

"More or less," said Hadley.

We had an hour to kill so Hadley suggested having a drink in the market. "That's beer—not coffee." She shuddered slightly.

We went to the Copacabana and sat out on the balcony. Two Tecates and a plate of ceviche. The sun was just going down and it was still surprisingly warm.

"It's too bad hats have gone out of style," I told Hadley as she arranged her long limbs in the small chair.

"There are times when you could look just like Virginia Woolf."

"Her cheekbones were nicer than mine."

"I love you anyway."

She smiled at me, and then looked troubled. "Peggy and Denise are coming back in three weeks," she said.

"I know. Have you thought anymore—about living together?"

"I've thought about it—I think about it a lot, but I don't know. It's not that I find it hard to live with you—sometimes I just wonder if I could live with anyone, give up my freedom."

"You want to sleep with someone else, don't you?"

"Don't jump to conclusions... All I'm saying is—you're a twin, you grew up under your sister's armpit, in each other's pockets. I've seen those kid pictures, the identical striped dresses, the same haircuts. You're used to having someone around all the time, it feels natural to you. But I was an only child, my parents were divorced, I've never stayed with anybody longer than two years."

"Are you getting restless already? It's only been eight months. You can't really count the summer before last."

"It's not you," she assured me. "You're not doing anything wrong. It's me—sometimes I feel cramped."

"Maybe it's the houseboat," I said. "We could get a bigger place, each have our own room."

Hadley drained her beer and looked out over the market below us. "I think it would be better," she said softly, "If we went back to each of us having our own place, Pam."

I felt tears at the back of my throat. I wanted to cry, "But I don't like to live alone, I'm lonely living alone. I always thought after October we'd find a house together, live happily ever after." Instead I said, rather stiffly, "We don't have to be monogamous either, if you don't want to."

I wanted her to tell me again not to jump to conclusions. That was why I said it. But Hadley only stared a little moodily off into the distance and said, "Well, maybe we should consider that."

When we got to the Frankfurter, Nicky was waiting for us, nondescript again in jeans, a black raincoat and with a black slouch hat over her curly hair. Only her eyes, with their false lashes and thick liner, connected her with the secret world of the Fun Palace. She was eating bockwurst and drinking a Pepsi.

"I only have half an hour," she said. She had a soft voice, a relaxed but slightly shy manner.

"Well," I said. "It's about Loie."

"Yes," she said. "I thought it might be." She looked at me with direct brown eyes and I found it harder than I'd thought to ask my questions. Maybe it would be better to lead up to it.

"What's it like?" I said. "Dancing at the Fun Palace?"

"It's different for different people, the same as any job. Did you watch us long?"

Hadley laughed. "Five dollars' worth."

"The other two women have more mixed feelings than I do. Shelley's like me, a student, and there for the money. The other one, Cyndi, has a lot of complicated emotional things going on and she says this is helping her work it out. She's the one who goes right up to the windows."

"You're a student?" I said.

"I'm finishing a Ph.D. in English Literature. I did all my course work at Stanford. Now I'm writing my thesis on Djuna Barnes. Shelley's in nursing school."

"Oh," Hadley and I said.

"Don't be embarrassed. I try to keep different parts of my life separate. I'd be in trouble at the university if people knew. Still, I expect I'd survive it. Meanwhile, dancing pays the rent and, I have to admit, I really enjoy it. It feels like a relief, after you've been reading and making notes, to take off your clothes and move and dance." Nicky looked at our faces. "It's so hopeless to try to explain one's particular form of sexuality; still, I find I'm always trying. I'm an exhibitionist really. I like to show off my body, to feel looked at, to play act. I always have and I don't feel there's anything wrong with it." She finished her bockwurst and smiled. "So what did you want to know from me?"

"Do you think—I mean, Loie and the dog collar—I mean, what I'm wondering is, would be possible to kill someone by tightening a dog collar on them?"

"It would be hard," said Nicky. "You'd have to use a lot of force. That's why I know Loie wasn't killed by anyone into S/M."

"Why not?"

"Because S/M isn't about force. It's about consent. About pushing someone up to and beyond what they think they can bear."

"Wouldn't it be easy to go past that point—to really hurt someone?"

"No. Because the first thing you learn when you start practicing S/M is the rules and how to do it safely. You don't do *anything* without the consent of the bottom. You agree on a word that means stop—a word that's not 'stop' or 'no'—a code word like 'mercy' or something. S/M is about the flowing of power back and forth between the top and the bottom—the top remains in control so that the bottom can feel out of control. She can scream 'No' and 'Stop' and have the top go right on. It's set up so the bottom can experience the sense of saying 'No,' and then being carried past it. S/M isn't about deliberately trying to *hurt* someone or being hurt. It's about exploring limits."

Nicky looked at us with a strange kind of passion. "So it couldn't have been someone into S/M who killed Loie. I know everyone in the community here. There's no one who would have a reason to strangle Loie at a conference. We were there to argue with her, not to murder her."

"You don't think that Loie... "

"Could have been involved in S/M? The idea's ludicrous. There was a time once when Loie was more adventurous, but now she makes—made—a living out of puritanism. She totally repressed that part of herself."

"What do you mean—'once'? Did you know her?"

Nicky hesitated. "I used to know her and Hanna. A long time ago. Neither of them have spoken to me for years."

She shrugged. "I've gotten used to it. People hating you because you refuse to repress something that they're trying desperately to squash down in themselves or pretend doesn't exist. In Loie's case, going so far as to construct an entire ideology around the things she was most afraid of seeing in herself. I figure it's not my problem except when it comes to censorship."

"At the workshop I went to, Loie talked about having had... rape fantasies, and being humiliated and degraded. Do you have any idea what she meant by that?"

A funny smile twisted at Nicky's lips. "Only Loie could know what she meant by that."

She got up to leave. Hadley said, "You're a good dancer. It was a pleasure watching you."

"Thanks," she said, pleased, and squared her small shoulders. "If there's nothing else?" she asked me.

There were still lots of unanswered questions, but I wasn't quite sure how far I could push Nicky. I wanted to ask her what had happened to the dog collar and leash she'd been wearing during the conference. I'd seen her put her hands up to it as if to take it off. Could she have given it to the person she was talking to? Was it her dog collar that had killed Loie? There were other questions too. I wanted to know if a leash could catch someone by surprise and choke them. And if Loie could have possibly arranged to see Nicky at any time during the conference, to discuss old times. I wondered if Nicky knew what Loie might have been about to say to the audience and what had stopped her from saying it.

But Nicky was halfway to the door, and something told me I should watch what I said. Nevertheless I couldn't help blurting out, "Who were you talking to outside the auditorium during Gracie's speech?"

Nicky turned and smiled at me, a dazzling, deceptive smile. "A theology student," she said. "Who wanted to save me."

8

Loie Marsh's memorial service was attended by a crowd that was more indignant than grieved. Loie had made her life into a cause; her death became one too. Hadley declined to go; she said she'd rather hang out with Ray at Best Printing and baby-sit Antonia. So Penny and I went together.

Neither of us had been to a service since our parents had died five years before. It was surprising how much the smell of flowers, the organ music, and the funereal mood brought back the shock and horror of that day. Penny clutched my hand as we filed into the funeral parlor and didn't let go of it through the ceremony. I tried to focus on what was going on; not to do so would have meant plunging back into a morass of loss and bereavement.

The funeral parlor was a large, very respectable one in the North End. Its middle-class opulence made me realize that I knew little or nothing about Loie's background and upbringing. Did she have parents and, if so, where were they? Down in the front pew was Hanna Sandbakker, wearing an elegant black dress and a stern expression; her ash-blond hair was pulled back into a low Greek knot. Next to her was the elderly, white-haired man I'd seen her with on the evening of the panel discussion. On Hanna's other side was a rather glamorous, heavy-set woman in her sixties and a much older woman, long-boned and graceful in a violet coat and hat. They must all be family. Almost everyone in the chapel was a woman, and most of them looked as if they'd been to the conference. Of course no sexual liberals were here, unless you counted me and Penny, and we were more like sexual mugwumps on the fence that divided the perverts from the puritans. I saw Elizabeth Ketteridge, but she didn't see me. One of these days I'd have to come to terms with the feelings it roused in me to run into her out of her office, and to see her no longer as a counselor but as an ordinary person whose views might well be different from mine. I also saw the therapist who'd been forced to come out as a former sadomasochist at Miko's workshop. Clea Florence, someone had said her name was.

Just as the ceremony was about to begin, someone came in the back and marched right up to where the family was sitting. The heavy-set woman didn't seem to want to make room for the newcomer; it was Hanna who slid over so she could sit down. Harried-looking, with flyaway beige hair and small, cramped features, the woman was carrying a flight bag. She'd obviously just arrived from somewhere, and in a hurry.

The ceremony began. Whoever the reverend was, he didn't have more than the vaguest of notions who Loie was. His little talk about her referred to her generous and forgiving nature, her untimely death in the flower of her youth and so on. He never once referred to the fact that Loie had been murdered and that even now her body could not be present at her own memorial service, as it was still at the morgue. He spoke instead with a meaningful air of Loie's enormous contribution to the welfare of society, her constant desire to put the needs of others first, her understanding of and patience with other people's viewpoints. (Penny couldn't help pinching my arm at that one.)

Afterwards, of course, there were grumblings.

"Why'd they have that guy?"

"An insult to everything Loie stood for."

"We should make our own memorial service. A women's service."

The main trouble was, nobody really knew Loie all that well. Which was strange, because until she'd moved to Boston and become famous eight or nine years ago, she'd spent her life in Seattle, had gone to the University of Washington, had worked presumably—what had she worked at?

I turned to a woman nearby. "Do you know what Loie did, before she moved to Boston?"

The woman shook her head. "That was before my time. I've only been in Seattle a couple of years."

"I know," said the woman next to her. "She taught drama at a high school in Kirkland, the same place my sister teaches. I think she was married. But I don't remember the man's name."

"Married?" someone gasped. A married high school teacher—even of drama—was certainly not what you thought of when you thought of Loie Marsh. Still, I supposed everyone experienced twists and turns in life. I wondered what had happened to the husband, and if he was here at the funeral.

The crowd was dispersing and Penny was off to talk to Hanna. From a distance I saw Hanna's beautifully defined profile lift gratefully in response to some question of Penny's. She looked exhausted.

I glanced around. The woman who'd come in late had moved from the front pew to a seat by herself in a corner. She was slumping over her flight bag, hugging it tightly to her thin chest.

"Are you Pauline?" I asked. "Loie's ex-lover?"

"'Ex-lover,'" she said bitterly, not looking up. "Is that what she told everyone here?"

"I'm sorry," I apologized. "She may not have said that at all. It's just something I heard."

"Don't try to make it better," Pauline said. "Loie

Marsh was in the process of dumping me. Everyone knew it except me. She told everyone except me. She didn't bother to tell me. Maybe she thought she had."

Pauline's voice was extraordinarily unpleasant. It sounded as if she had a cold, but I suspected it might be more permanent than that. Either adenoids or sinus trouble.

"When did you find out?" I asked.

"I wasn't the first one anyone called," Pauline said. "That's clear. Eight years Loie and I were together, lived together seven years and that horror of a mother of hers didn't even bother to phone. It was Hanna who called me about the memorial service." Tears began to fall down Pauline's faintly wrinkled cheeks. "Some people in Boston knew right away, right after Loie was killed. But did anyone tell me? Oh no. No, I helped Loie with her speeches, I practically wrote her book for her, I did all the research for the new book, I made Loie what she was—but did anyone bother to tell me she'd been murdered?"

"Everyone probably thought you knew," I tried to comfort her. "I'm sure you're terribly upset."

"Me?" said Pauline. And there was a frightening smirk on her cramped features when she raised her head. "I'm glad the bitch is dead, if you want to know the truth."

And, clutching her flight bag, she stumbled past me and out the door, bumping into people along the way.

I went over to Penny and Hanna. "Oh, Pauline," said Hanna, her velvet voice hardening, when I asked her if she really hadn't known about Loie's murder. "By the end of their relationship Pauline had gotten so paranoid about Loie getting the jump on her in everything, that she was ready to believe that Loie had gotten herself killed just so she could die first." Hanna tried to smile. "I'm sorry. That's really bad taste. Of course Pauline's upset. But my aunt said she did call Pauline right after it happened Saturday night. It may be just that Pauline was too upset to take it in. When I called her yesterday to tell her about the service all I got was her message machine. She didn't return my call so I didn't think she'd turn up. But she did and now she's angry with all of us."

"I hate to pry," I said. "But are you sure they'd really broken up?"

"According to Loie, it had all been over months ago. Pauline had just refused to believe it." Hanna sighed tiredly. "I hope she's not going to make a big fuss and hang around Seattle. I suppose she's going to want some of Loie's things—that's only natural." Hanna touched a graceful hand to her forehead and suddenly I was caught by her look of absolute sorrow. Here I'd been thinking her rather callow—now I saw her wretchedness. Or her impersonation of wretchedness?

"Has there been any progress with, with... ?" Penny couldn't quite say it.

"With finding the one who did it, you mean? No, not really. One of the problems is that Loie just wasn't in Seattle long enough. If she had enemies they're most likely in Boston."

"Unless it was someone she'd tangled with here before," I said. "Like maybe her ex-husband?"

"What do you know about her ex-husband?" Hanna's fine eyebrows drew together.

"Just something someone said. . . . " I trailed off. "But you're right, it must have been someone from Boston, someone who... "

Penny took my arm. "We really should be going."

"Wait," said Hanna, almost desperately. Loie's mother came over. She was wearing a dark wool suit and rather flashy clip earrings. She looked like a woman who owned her own business, something small but not tacky—flowers perhaps, or Hallmark cards. Her face was like Loie's, fleshy, somewhat swollen. Her auburn hair was most certainly a wig.

"Hanna, dear," she announced. "We're all coming over to your place. Granny simply must lie down after all this excitement and your house is closest."

"It's a mess, Aunt Edith."

"Nonsense, darling. At a time like this who could possibly care?" Loie's mother included us in her wave, "Come along, come along."

We found ourselves being herded into Mrs. Marsh's late model Ford sedan. Mrs. Sandbakker was in the front seat, absolutely silent, and Mrs. Marsh drove. Hanna and her father were coming in another car.

"Shocking, shocking," said Mrs. Marsh, when Penny and I expressed our condolences. "Twenty years ago there was absolutely no crime in this city. Now it's everywhere. Brutal, random violence. It's drug addicts, there are drug addicts everywhere nowadays."

"So you don't think it could have been anyone Loie knew?"

Mrs. Marsh stared at us in the rear view mirror. "Knew? With Loie so prominent as a feminist? How could Loie know a drug addict? Loie was far too clean-living. None of us could be pure enough for her. She loathed the idea that her widowed mother might even think of sex, much less have it from time to time. She couldn't bear me wearing make-up or heels, and if I was watching *Dallas* on TV she'd come over and give me a lecture. My dear, a woman like that isn't murdered by anyone she knows—she couldn't know anyone capable of such a crime. No, it just means that the drug situation in Seattle is getting worse and worse. It's terribly frightening, absolutely terrifying. What's that, Mother?"

The straight-backed old woman had said something under her breath.

"We can't hear you, Mother."

In a slight Norwegian accent, Mrs. Sandbakker said, "I think maybe Loie did something to deserve it... maybe."

"Mother!" Mrs. Marsh cut her off. "How can you say such a thing! Of course Loie didn't deserve to be a victim of random violence. It's so ironic, so horribly ironic when you compare the murder statistics in Boston and Seattle and think that it had to happen here. Of course Loie couldn't have *done* anything to deserve it."

But I wondered.

Hanna's house was a crisply painted wooden frame in a large lot that had been recently and probably professionally landscaped—hence its bare, almost ascetic look in contrast to the others on the street, which were filled to the brim with dahlias and roses. In Hanna's yard there were small, unusual looking bushes, a lot of gravel and nothing in flower at all. The neighborhood was in Ballard, where most of the Scandinavians had settled in Seattle. Although inevitably newcomers had moved in, looking for housing bargains and predominantly white schools, Market Street was the only place in Seattle where you could still hear people speaking Norwegian, Danish or Swedish, and Johnsen's Scandinavian Foods still the best place to go if you were looking for cardamom rolls, pickled herring or bars of Freia's chocolate. King Olav of Norway himself had dedicated the little town square.

Of course Hanna's house wasn't a mess at all when we arrived. With its polished wood floors, woven rugs on the walls and clean-smelling pine furniture it looked like many homes I'd been to in my youth. Like thousands of people in Seattle Penny and I had Norwegians in our closet. Our great-grandfather, Harald Nilsen, had been born in Stavanger, had made his way over by boat to Seattle and had run a thriving dry goods store in Ballard. Later generations had drifted over to the University District and Ravenna and the dry goods store had become a hardware store and then a pet shop; still, some of the old customs had remained. Our father had been (to our great embarrassment) a member of the Sons of Norway and had liked to eat brown goat cheese on buttered rolls for lunch and fish in white sauce with potatoes for dinner. He'd always celebrated the 17th of May, Norway's Constitution Day, with Aquavit and herring and *kransekake*, a tall pyramid of hard, anise-flavored coils. He'd shepherded the family to Norway once and always dreamed of spending another vacation sailing the fjords. Our mother, who had some Norwegian relatives still living in Telemark but who was mainly a confused blend of Irish-Scottish-German, thought the whole thing about the old country was far too sentimental. She always said she'd rather cruise the Amazon than the Gjeranger Fjord.

She never would now. He never would now.

It must have been the atmosphere of death in the house, like a thin layer of dust over everything, that made me feel as if I were going to cry. I didn't know why we were here with these strangers on such a private occasion.

Hanna dragged Penny into the kitchen to help her make coffee and I was left in the living room with the relatives. An awkward silence sat down with us.

"It was a good service," said Hanna's father. He had a quiet deep voice, a kind but distracted look. "I thought a very good service. Lots of people."

"I don't know, Erik," said Mrs. Marsh. "There were a lot of people I expected to see there that I didn't. David, for instance."

"Well, he's remarried, you know. I wouldn't suppose he'd come if he's remarried. Didn't he send flowers? That's all you can expect, if he's remarried."

"And that Pauline," Mrs. Marsh continued. "Making such a scene, coming late like that."

"Yes," Erik Sandbakker said. "Hardly considerate. But it was a very good service. I don't think we could have expected David to come. Now that he's remarried."

"It's not that I minded Loie turning into a you-know," said Mrs. Marsh. "But Pauline is just too hopeless for words. I don't really understand what she and Loie had in common. Loie was so clever, publishing that book and getting all that attention." She suddenly turned to me, her chest inflating under her wool suit, "You know she was on Phil Donahue once, dear." Then she continued, "My opinion is that Pauline resented Loie awfully. There are a lot of people who resented Loie when she was growing up—Loie was so bright and big for her age. She could talk at one, she was reading when she was four. Why, you resented Loie sometimes, didn't you, Hanna?" she asked her niece, who was carrying a very Scandinavian-looking tray with a red ceramic matching coffee service and some kind of biscuits—oat cakes, I bet—layered with thin, caramel-colored strips of goat cheese.

Hanna blanched slightly. "Whatever makes you say that, Aunt Edith? Loie and I were *years* apart, our interests were completely different." She set the tray down with a crack and poured the coffee.

"Only three years apart, darling," Edith Marsh remonstrated. "The two of you were so sweet together, remember Erik? Hanna would follow Loie around like her little slave, remember?"

"She was so bossy," Hanna muttered.

"It was Hanna who gave Loie her name." Mrs. Marsh's large face had gone soft and she looked at Hanna as if she were looking at a little girl. "Because Hanna couldn't pronounce Chloe. You could hear her following Loie around, crying in that dear little voice of hers, 'Loie, Loie, where are you Loie?'"

"*Please*, Aunt Edith," Hanna said, but her aunt went on, tears welling in her eyes,

"Don't you remember that time, Erik, when the two families went to the ocean and little Hanna got completely out of her depth in the water and Loie marched right in— she was only seven but she was so big for her age—and she plucked Hanna up and dragged her to the shore. Saved her life really."

"Don't, Aunt Edith! Please don't." Like an overwrought heroine, Hanna had collapsed over a chair and was sobbing wildly. "Not today! I really can't bear it."

Everyone got up in consternation and went over to her. I took it to mean that Penny and I should quietly depart and leave them to their memories.

We slipped out.

9

DEATH WAS SOMETHING Penny and I never talked about. We hadn't talked about it since that day five years ago when the phone had rung unexpectedly in each of our homes and the police had informed us both that our parents had died in a head-on collision. Instantly orphans at an age when most people we knew were just beginning to re-evaluate their adolescent and post-adolescent family quarrels and allegiances, we lost ourselves in details about the house and the business so we wouldn't have to mourn.

So much was still painful. Like my knowing that Penny had always been Dad's favorite, two minutes older than me but for all that the biggest, the brightest, the bossiest. Dad thought she could do anything and, in his eyes, she could. I compensated by growing smaller and weaker so I could really be the little sister and take my place in the family cosmology. I was a reader, and often sick. I was Mama's baby, and some of the happiest days of my childhood were spent at home, with a not very bad sore throat and a pile of Nancy Drews.

Penny knew that I used to hate my father sometimes, and maybe that was why we didn't speak of him much now. We were far likelier to talk about our mother, when we talked about our parents at all. Yet Dad's absence left a hole in Penny's life. He'd always been there to applaud her social and scholastic successes. He'd expected the world of her; when she started studying biochemistry he'd immediately expressed his belief that she'd win the Nobel prize someday. I knew she felt terribly sad he would never know she'd married a nice man and had a baby daughter.

If our parents had lived it's quite likely that Penny and I would have gone our separate ways, meeting for holidays and special occasions. One or the other of us might have moved away from Seattle; it probably would have been Penny. The irony and the wonder of our parent's death is that it pushed us together into an intimacy we'd only had as young children. We'd taken over their printing business, we'd immediately moved together into their house. We'd been each other's support and mainstay, because it was so clear: *We were all we had left.*

But during the last year things had changed. Our differences at the moment seemed so much more apparent than our connections. Although on the surface Penny appeared much more actively political than I was, I saw her trip to Nicaragua as having reinforced her role as a responsible citizen. Perhaps that was unfair; perhaps I felt guilty for not having gone myself. The real issue between us was conventionality. It was as if we had resurrected childish roles—Penny the Meeter-of-Expectations. Pam the Secret Rebel. I knew Penny didn't really accept my becoming a lesbian, just as I didn't really accept her becoming a wife and mother.

And we still never talked about death.

"What's Hanna really like?" I asked Penny as we made our way down to Market Street in search of a bus that would take us back to the funeral home to pick up our cars.

"It's funny," Penny said meditatively. "That scene in there reminded me a little of our first day in Nicaragua. I mean, her crying. We'd just gotten to the hotel and everyone was exhausted but excited, Hanna more than most. She had always been a very strong supporter of the Sandinistas, was really eager to go there, to work. And then we got there, unpacked, were just ready to go down to have dinner—and she completely cracked. She started crying and kind of raking at her arms like that, and saying she didn't know why she was here, she wasn't supposed to be here—things that really didn't make sense."

"But crying because your cousin has been murdered and because your aunt reminds you she saved your life when you were four or five—surely that calls for extreme emotion."

"Of course it does," agreed Penny. "I'm just saying there's something that reminds me—like an almost hysterical, out-of-control self-hatred—I don't know. Someone gave her a tranquilizer that night in Managua and the rest of the six weeks she was absolutely great. She worked very hard, her Spanish was brilliant, she was good-tempered and so on. It was just that first night."

"Did anything—anyone—say anything to set her off?"

"I don't think so." Penny shook her head. "Or if they did, it seemed so trivial that I didn't remember it."

Penny had to go back to the print shop and feed Antonia but I decided to take the rest of the day off. I'd been shaken by the whole experience—the service, Loie's family, Hanna breaking down, Pauline's bitterness. I decided to go up to the Espressomat and talk to Hadley. Maybe she'd have some ideas about where to go from here and whether I should even be pursuing any of this.

Hadley was still at Best Printing they told me when I came in, but they were expecting her soon. I took a copy of an old *off our backs* over to a table by the window and sat down with a decaf mocha. One of the great advantages to being Hadley's girlfriend was that I got my coffee free.

It was a pleasant, quiet afternoon. I read about women's struggles in different parts of the world for a while, then turned to the letters page. There was one from a woman prisoner, another from an author who disagreed with a review of her novel and one from Loie Marsh. It was brief and to the point—she disassociated herself completely from an article published about her in a women's magazine. The writer had never contacted Loie directly, but had pieced the article together from second-hand reports from other people and other sources. She especially wanted to say that she had never said that the American Civil Liberties Union was entirely composed of sadomasochists:

"Probably no more than half are into S/M."

Suddenly I jumped up and dashed out the door. A familiar figure had just crossed the street and was heading down the block. I might not have recognized her features, but I could certainly remember the set of those hunched hurrying shoulders. She was still carrying her flight bag.

"Pauline," I called after her.

She jumped like a cat whose tail has been stepped on and almost hissed.

"What do you want?"

"I'm Pam—I talked to you at the service this morning. I thought you might like a cup of coffee." I gestured to the Espressomat.

"Well," Pauline hesitated. Her slumping was probably habitual but her evident exhaustion made it worse; her neck had practically disappeared. Her face looked like a crumpled piece of paper someone had balled up and thrown away. "I could use a cup of something. Tea."

I took her back with me to the cafe and ordered her a pot of Earl Grey.

"You must be feeling pretty rocky," I sympathized, only partly with ulterior motives. She did look like she needed a friendly ear. "Do you feel like talking about it?"

"I don't know," she said, pushing her stringy beige hair out of her pinched little face. "I don't know what I'm doing, just walking around. Do you realize that this is the first time I've been in Seattle? Loie and I were together eight years and this is the first time I've ever seen where she grew up. It's so typical somehow."

"You two must have gotten together fairly soon after Loie left Seattle."

"We did," said Pauline and for a moment she permitted herself a small smile. "I met her right after she'd moved, at the first Boston Women Against Pornography meeting she came to. She swept me off my feet. . . She had so much *conviction.*"

Pauline sighed nasally. "Loie immediately became our main speaker. I helped her write her talks and speeches. She was nervous at first, she said she was a better performer than a writer—she used to be able to joke about it. Then people said she should write articles. I helped her with them too. Then an agent came long and asked if she'd ever thought of writing a book. Up to then we hadn't thought—I hadn't thought—of 'mine' and 'yours.' It was for the cause of women against violence against women, it didn't matter who said it first.

"That was my idealism—then. I knew better than anyone that Loie's thinking was muddled, that she couldn't organize her thoughts, that her logic was faulty. She was naturally dramatic, though, and she could be so. . . moving. Me, on the other hand—I'm a clear, rational thinker. I did the rewording, the rewriting, the polishing. They were all, the articles and the speeches, joint efforts. When the book was suggested, Loie asked for my help. The way she explained it was that it really didn't matter whose name was on the cover, that the agent had only come to Loie after hearing her speak, that everyone would know my ideas were equally valid and that naturally we'd split the royalty income from the book." Pauline grimaced. "Naive, wasn't I?"

"Did you split the royalties?"

"Well, we lived together and shared expenses. Meaning, Loie lived with me and I supported her on my teacher's salary—I used to teach English at a private girls' school. We had a joint checking account anyway—so the advance and the first couple of years of royalties went right into that account. At first it was wonderful. We bought a house and I quit my job to manage Loie's career. I knew it was Loie's name that sold the book—as well as the fact she went on the talk shows and did so well. I could *never* have been interviewed on TV. I would have died of nervousness. But I still got to travel with Loie and meet people and participate in the movement."

Pauline lifted the lid of the teapot and stared at the sodden Earl Grey dregs. "I didn't realize the extent to which the feminist movement is a product of the media. Lots of movement women claim not to be part of the patriarchal, capitalist structure—to have developed alternative values. Bullshit! Feminism is a word and image based construction like anything else—it thrives on symbols—it makes people into symbols and people make themselves into symbols to accommodate it.

"Once Loie had her name on *The Silenced Heart* she was automatically a more valuable person than I was. Once Loie had been on the Phil Donahue Show or asked to be a keynote speaker at the National Women's Studies Conference she was a star. She was asked again. And again. I became known as Loie's manager—not her lover, not publicly—while Loie became known as one of the founders of the anti-pornography movement. Once she'd said that everyone would know how much I'd contributed to the book. How the hell were they going to know that? In the beginning, the very beginning, she used to mention me in her interviews and talks and say, 'I couldn't have done it without Pauline Corot.' 'Pauline Corot's ideas are an essential part of my book.' But gradually references to my contribution got fewer and fewer. When the royalties began to slow down and the invitations dried up, suddenly *I* was supposed to get a job to keep up the mortgage payments. She acted as if *she'd* been supporting *me*."

Pauline's lips pressed together savagely.

"If you don't mind my asking, why did you come all the way out here to her memorial service?"

Pauline looked surprised and hurt. "Loie Marsh was my lover for eight years. She was my life."

But I had begun to wonder if her visit had anything to do with the manuscript Loie had been working on.

"I suppose you had lots of input into the new book too, didn't you?"

"It was totally based on my research," said Pauline. "For years I'd been keeping notes on meetings that we went to, and saving clippings. At first it was going to be a joint project—the history of the anti-pornography movement. I was the one who came up with the title—*We Took Back the Night*. But about six months ago Loie took the project over herself. She signed a contract and put the advance into a separate checking account. She refused to talk about it, except when she felt like taunting me with trying to cash in on her success, with being jealous of her. I'm sure she broke up with me just because she felt guilty for stealing all my ideas. And I know she told everyone lies about me too."

"But surely people didn't believe what she said. I mean—Loie does have a reputation for being difficult."

"She can be—could be—completely convincing if that's what she wanted. And most people *did* know her as the author of *The Silenced Heart*."

"What was Loie's relationship to her family?"

Again Pauline pressed her lips together in disgust. "In her speeches she always talked about it being a matriarchy—three generations of women and all that—but in actual fact I don't think she liked her family all that much. Except for Hanna. She adored Hanna."

"She did?"

"Oh yes. They were really close as kids. But somewhere along the line they had a falling out about something. I was never sure what, I always assumed it was radical feminist politics versus leftist politics. Hanna is a real peacenik. Loie was always hoping she could convert her."

"What about Loie's ex-husband?"

"What do you mean—ex-husband?"

I stumbled under the glare of Pauline's eyes. "I... I heard she'd been married."

"That's ridiculous," Pauline snapped. "She's always been a lesbian, she told me."

"Oh." I didn't know what else to say. Pauline looked dangerously angry.

"That would really be the last straw," she muttered, getting up to leave, looking around for her flight bag.

I tried desperately to think of how I could ask her whether Loie could have been involved in S/M (without implying that Pauline was S or M herself), whether Loie had the kind of enemies in Boston who might have wished her dead or even where I could get hold of Pauline if I needed to. But Pauline was already halfway out the door, still muttering, "Married!"

I watched her stride across the street as if she knew where she was going, then I decided to visit the local bookstore and get a copy of *The Silenced Heart*. But the bookstore didn't have a copy. As was the case with a number of feminist classics from the seventies the mass market edition had gone out of print. I was advised to try the used bookstore down the street. There I found a hardcover copy, rather dog-eared and embellished with quotes on the back cover from Steinem, Chesler and Dworkin, all more or less saying that this book was going to blow off everybody's socks.

On the way back to the Espressomat I was struck by an odd thought. I wondered if I should call Loie's mother and ask if Loie had made a will. I even thought of asking Hanna to keep an eye on Loie's boxes of research materials and on the manuscript of *We Took Back the Night*.

I didn't call because I didn't have a quarter on me, and because I thought they might think I was meddling too much.

I suppose things wouldn't have turned out too much differently if I had.

10

I SPENT THE LATE afternoon and early evening reading *The Silenced Heart*. Hadley had said she wouldn't be home for dinner, that she was going out to a movie. Since our conversation a couple of days ago about living together and monogamy—or rather, non-monogamy— explaining what we were doing and who we were going to do it with had become an area of some tension. "I'm going out with a friend," Hadley had said on the phone. Instead of casually asking who or challenging her or even acted wounded, I merely replied, "See you later."

I sat out on the floating dock and watched the twin towers of the Montlake drawbridge, the ones that looked a little like European castles, until it got too cold. Then I went inside and lay on the sofa. Soon I was engrossed in Loie's book, in her righteous indignation, in her (or Pauline's) vivid and furious prose. No doubt about it, women were much angrier a while back, with an anger that didn't allow for complexities, that burned away all the scrub—and many of the trees—and left you looking at a world you'd never seen before.

Men hated women. Always had. Always would. There was absolutely no other way to explain history, no other way to explain why men had triumphed and women had failed, why men's accomplishments were plastered everywhere and women's were swept under the rug. Men hated women—who knew why—and this was nowhere more apparent than in the field of sexuality. In fact, the way men enforced their domination over women was through sexuality, through sexual violence.

This was all in Loie's introduction. The succeeding chapters hammered the message home with details; from footbinding to rape to marriage to pornography, history was a horrific war waged by men against women.

There had been other writers, before and since Loie, who had discussed many of these problems, writers by the carload who had variously laid the oppression of women by men down to psychological, biological or economic causes. Anthropologists, poets and politicians had all put in their two cents at one time or another. But nobody I'd ever read came quite as close as Loie did to capturing men's rage against women and to setting up a counter-rage: of despair, anger, militancy.

I couldn't finish the book, though it wasn't a long one. My teeth were almost chattering with fury by the end of Chapter Three. I was experiencing a new kind of respect for Loie. The wonder wasn't that she'd been killed, but that she hadn't been killed before this.

I got up, did my sit-ups and push-ups and wished I had the punching bag from the gym right here. I did some kicks and turns and made some fierce noises. Then I rooted around for my address book and called Elizabetth Ketteridge. I got the answering machine.

Frustrated, I said, more vehemently than necessary, "Elizabeth this is Pam Nilsen. I really *need* to talk to you," and then was taken aback when her smoothly modulated voice came on the line, "Hello Pam."

"Oh, hi," I said. "Listen, can I possibly come over?"

"I'm just finishing some things at the office," Elizabeth hesitated. "I really shouldn't be home late. Couldn't we possibly make an early appointment for, say... sometime the beginning of October?"

"It's not about me," I said, though that wasn't really true. "It's about Loie. There are some things I want to know about her."

Maybe Elizabeth wanted, or needed, to talk about Loie too. She appeared to be thinking. Finally she said, "I'll call Nan and tell her I'll be late. But I can only spare a half hour or so."

"I'll be right over."

Elizabeth's office was in Wallingford, across the University Bridge and not far from the houseboat. I hadn't been there since the end of last May when I'd stopped seeing her. It was starting to rain a little when I pulled up in front of the house that had been turned into various offices. I remembered how I used to climb these stairs every week last spring. At first it had been with a kind of dread in my stomach that I was going to have to talk about *it* and how I couldn't seem to get over *it* and about how I'd had another dream about *it*. Afterwards I'd walk down the stairs, sometimes crying and shaking. As the weeks went on things got easier to talk about. The nicest time with Elizabeth was right before the end, when we used to sit and have a cup of tea and talk about my blossoming affair with Hadley, my sister's pregnancy.

Now, only four months later, the bloom seemed to be fading on the relationship with Hadley, Antonia had been born and I felt excluded from my sister's life, and I was walking up the stairs, after having read Loie's book, with some of the same sensations of murderous rage I'd experienced in the middle of my course of therapy.

Elizabeth came to the door, looking fragile and bulbous, like an onion or an iris. She motioned me to sit down and said in a professional voice, "Now, what about Loie can I help you with?"

"I've just been reading her book," I began. "I never read it before."

"Ah!"

"Yes, some of it is upsetting to me. But it's also made me start thinking about Loie's death in a different way."

Elizabeth placed her fingertips together. "What way?"

"I think I've—most of us—have been operating under the assumption that Loie's killer is someone from Seattle, someone who killed her for so far unknown reasons specifically at the conference. To either make a point or to cause a scandal. Maybe to implicate Loie in S/M. Maybe to stop her from speaking on the panel. But what if the murderer was someone who'd hated Loie for a long time and just used this opportunity to make it look as if it were connected with the conference?"

"It's possible," said Elizabeth. Her large eyes looked at me uneasily.

"What I'm wondering," I said, "is how long you've known Loie and if you knew her in Seattle before she went to Boston?"

"I *did* know her then," said Elizabeth hesitantly. "It was at a time when I was just getting involved in the whole issue of rape and violence against women. Up to then I'd been approaching rape and sexual abuse on a very piecemeal basis. I was finishing my degree in clinical psychology—my subject was depression in women, and I knew that some depressed women had been sexually molested. Then I went to the slide show that Loie organized. I started reading—Susan Brownmiller, Andrea Dworkin, Phyllis Chesler, Susan Griffin. Overnight my life changed. I stopped being interested in treating depression medically and got interested in treating it politically. A lot of things happened that year. I got involved with Rape Relief where I met Nan. I became a lesbian. I began to redefine myself as a feminist therapist."

I was touched that she was opening up to me. I hadn't known any of this when I'd been seeing her.

"So then Loie was a friend of yours?"

Elizabeth shook her head. "Not exactly. I suppose I was a little in awe of her at first. And then she left."

"Do you know who her friends were?"

"She was always close to Hanna. . . . " Elizabeth hesitated again, and for some reason the thought flashed through my mind that she was protecting Loie somehow. Loie couldn't have been a client of hers, could she? "Loie was always a little bit of mystery. My sense of her is that she was probably a tormented person inside."

"Tormented?" I asked. "By what?"

Elizabeth stared at the church of her fingers again. "It didn't have an obvious cause, at least not one she ever talked about. But she could well have been a survivor or a witness of some form of sexual abuse. Clearly pornography was deeply upsetting to her. You do have to wonder if there was anything in particular that triggered it."

"Her father's dead, I think. I met her mother and her grandmother at the memorial service and they seemed very conventional. And her uncle, Hanna's father, seemed pretty harmless."

"I don't think we can psychoanalyze her on the basis of relatives who *seem* nice." Elizabeth smiled for the first time.

"I noticed that she talked about being betrayed a lot," I said. "By the sexual liberals mostly, but it felt like it went deeper."

"Oh, I wouldn't read too much into that," said Elizabeth. "It's the times. Everyone is so polarized about pornography, you can hardly help but take sides."

"But you don't seem so violently on the anti-porn side," I said.

"It's not my nature to show my feelings in the same way as Loie, perhaps. But I feel very strongly that pornography does have a causal relationship to violence against women. I agree in fact with Andrea Dworkin that porn *is* violence against women, it's not something separate that causes it. It's all part of the same social system. As women we *are* terrorized by the proliferation of porn. I know sex offenders and I know the way they think. It's frankly quite scary to think of all the men out there looking at violent videos, poring over magazines and thinking about ways they could act out the things they see and read. It's not about being a prude—I like my body, I love sex—it's about being scared. And I'm angry that I have to live my life scared."

I looked at Elizabeth and the feeling of trusting her more than anyone else on earth came over me again.

"I'm angry that it just goes on and on, that pornography proliferates and that nobody knows how to stop it. Beause I have to deal with the consequences. That's my work, listening to women who've been attacked and molested by men who believe they have the right to do it. Well, you know, Pam. You know."

"Yes," I said. "I know."

She said she'd walk out with me. On the sidewalk we stood for a minute. I felt I was towering over her. I never remembered her being as short as she was.

"Are you really doing all right, Pam?" she asked. "We could make an appointment for October. Or I could refer you to someone."

"Let me think about it," I said. "I have a lot going on right now, but some of it I just have to work out myself."

"Okay," she said, and touched my arm. "I hope I told you what you wanted to know about Loie."

"Thanks," I said, still with the strong impression she was hiding something.

I was back into Loie's book when Hadley returned home. She was humming as she hung up her jacket, completely oblivious to all the outrages perpetrated on us, on womankind.

"Margaret and I saw a great movie," she said, and named a romantic comedy-thriller that was currently very popular. "Really pleasant and old-fashioned: they meet, they fight, they reconcile. Very satisfying."

I looked up sternly from my book. "It's beyond me how you could enjoy a film that just reinforces the heteropatriarchy. I've seen the previews for that film. So what if the woman is a district attorney? It's just a set-up to make it more titillating when the woman is saved by the jerky hero."

Hadley looked at me in amazement and her wide mouth settled into a kind of frown. "Where's this coming from?" She peered at the title in my hand. "Oh-oh—the wrath of Loie Marsh lives on."

"It's true what she says, you know. That men hate women—at every historical period, in every possible way."

Hadley threw her long body onto the sofa across from me. "She makes a convincing argument, I'll say that for her. That book had an incredibly galvanizing effect on people. But it's outdated. For one thing she treats sexuality as if it were an unchanging paradigm: man screws woman in order to humiliate her. According to her men and women never act any differently. Whereas in fact there is an incredible amount of deviance from that model. Men fucking other men, women fucking other women, trans-sexuals, fetishists, celibates, bisexuals, women who dominate men and men who like being dominated. Loie left out all the interesting bits. She didn't even put in lesbians, and she's one herself. And even if you accept Loie's main idea—men hate women—leaving aside the question of whether you can prove it or not—where are you going to go from there? If it's always been like this and is always going to be like this, then what's the point of trying to change specific things? You might as well kill yourself."

"No, you don't. You can fight back!"

Hadley sighed and examined her nails. "Yeah. Fight Back! Take Back the Night! Get Your Asses Out in the Street! To the Barricades, Womyn!... And then what? Not to sound a discouraging note, but politics, government and so on is slightly more complicated. I'm not convinced that the women who write some of these books would be my favorite choice as president. Or queen. I'm sure some of them would like to be queen."

"But we need people who can make us feel how intolerable things are. Otherwise we just accept it."

"Which is precisely the attraction of activists like Loie. They're fine as long as they're trying to inspire revolt and change—it's when they get specific, if they ever do, about how they're going to institute change that you realize that some of their ideas sound pretty feeble and/or fascist."

My enthusiasm for the book was beginning to leak away slightly under Hadley's criticism and I remembered my conversation with Pauline. Was a woman who stole someone else's ideas and took all the credit for herself such a model for women of the future?

"I just don't want to write off Loie's sincerity," I said finally. "It's too easy just to see her as some kind of power-hungry fanatic who had a lot of enemies. But at her best she really cared deeply about women and she had a tremendous effect on the whole feminist movement."

I looked challengingly at Hadley but she seemed to have lost interest in arguing.

"What'd you do tonight?" she asked and came over to sit next to me.

"I went to see Elizabeth Ketteridge. I had some questions about Loie."

"Find out anything?"

"It's the same thing everywhere. Nobody really seems to have known her in Seattle. Still, I couldn't help feeling that Elizabeth knew something she didn't want to tell me."

"I've always liked Elizabeth," Hadley offered. "Was it nice to see her again?"

"Yes," I said. "Only... Hadley, sometimes it just comes back to me. Something sets it off and the whole thing just comes back. And in a way seeing Elizabeth is like that. It reminds me." I couldn't help it, I started crying a little.

Hadley held me. She'd held me before and would keep holding me for a while, I hoped.

11

JUNE AND I WENT to sit in a nearby park for lunch the next day and as we unwrapped our tuna sandwiches, I told her about reading Loie's book and talking to Elizabeth.

"Hadley's skeptical, but sometimes I think Elizabeth and Loie may be right. Pornography is about male power. It's very harmful to its audience and to the people who pose for the photographs and make the movies."

"A blow job is better than no job, as Margo St. James once said." June chewed on a pickle. "Seriously, Pam, I probably feel just as put off by porn as you do. I know Eddy used to look at it. We had a discussion and he stopped, but I wonder sometimes if he still does. It's such a male activity. That bothers me. You get the feeling that you're living in another universe. But I try to keep it in perspective. If this country has a national problem, it's drugs, not porn."

"Maybe they go together."

"Maybe they do, maybe they don't. They're about money, that's for sure. And some people are making a fortune off them."

"True," I said, thinking of the prices of magazines and videos at The Vault, which certainly didn't reflect the cost of the materials and labor that went into producing them. "Make something illicit and you can charge what you want for it. High prices only make people think it's more desirable."

"You ever think that's why some of these feminists are publishing sex magazines? They're defending our civil liberties all the way to the bank."

We finished our sandwiches and sat watching the waterfall in the corner of the little park. It was the first of October but the afternoon sun was very warm. June was sensibly dressed in a bright orange tee-shirt that brought out the coppery tones of her skin. I was sweating in a long-sleeved shirt.

June said, "I don't really feel the anti-porn movement has had much to say to the black community so far. They just use us when they want to compare censoring racist material to censoring porn."

"But what about Alice Walker and Audre Lorde? They've spoken out against S/M."

"Maybe because S/M is an especially hard issue for black women. When you've got a history of slavery in the not so distant past you're not real thrilled about the idea of pretending to be slave and mistress. It cuts too near the bone to be thinking about wearing leg irons—or even putting leg irons on somebody else."

We sat in silence a moment, then June said, "So, are you any closer to figuring out who killed Loie Marsh?"

I shook my head. "I've run through everybody in the panel in my mind. I can't believe that any of them had a reason to kill her. I see them all so clearly waiting to go on stage, they couldn't have been out in the bushes with a dog collar. Gracie and Miko were talking, Elizabeth was sitting there with her lover... "

"What about Sonya?"

"I guess I didn't know what she looked like before she came on stage. She could have been late. Nicky was also late, I remember. But we'd seen her and Oak in the restaurant. How would they have had time to kill Loie? That leaves Hanna, Loie's cousin, who also came in late, but with her father."

"Well?"

"But what would any of their motives be? The only one I can see who had a really obvious motive is Pauline, her ex-lover. Loie had left her and had taken all the research materials for a book they'd worked on together. But Pauline wasn't in Seattle the night of the murder. She was in Boston because Mrs. Marsh talked to her."

"What about people you don't know?"

"That's the trouble, I don't know any of her friends or enemies from Boston... and she had an ex-husband too. And all of a sudden everyone looks and sounds suspicious to me. For instance, I heard Loie and someone arguing after Loie's workshop. I don't know who it was, but it sounded as if Loie was planning to reveal something that the other woman didn't want her to reveal. I didn't recognize the voice—it could have been anybody."

June stood up and stretched. "I'm supposed to go over and see Gracie tonight," she said. "Maybe you want to come with me? You could check her out, maybe ask her some questions. But she'll talk your ear off, I'm warning you."

Before going to Gracie's however, there was something else I thought I should do, and that was stop by a planning meeting for the Loie March, as some people were already calling it. This was to be an enormous Take Back the Night march in honor of Loie and her fight against pornography. All the staunchest anti-porn activists were going to be there and I thought this might be an opportunity to ask a few more questions.

It was being held at the downtown YWCA. June declined to accompany me and I agreed to pick her up at nine to visit Gracie.

The room was packed with a combination of long-time activists with many agenda-setting and task-division skills

98

and a crowd of women, many of whom were in tears of fury, rage and abandonment over Loie's death. They were the women who had read and discussed *The Silenced Heart* in their Women's Studies classes; they were the generation who had come out as feminists and lesbian feminists at a time when the Women Against Violence Against Women movement was burgeoning and consciousness about rape, incest and sexual harassment was at its peak. These women didn't see Loie as human, but as their hero, their martyr. They didn't just want a march in her honor, they wanted to rename a downtown street for her; they wanted to dedicate a park or a building to her memory; they wanted to pull down the statue of George Washington on campus and put up one of Loie instead.

"Let's just start with the march for now," suggested Elizabeth Ketteridge's lover, Nan, who was chairing the meeting. "Now, who can make posters?"

"I think we should occupy the Mayor's office," interrupted an earnest woman in jeans and a checked shirt. "Until there's a full-scale investigation of Loie's murder. Obviously there's been a conspiracy and we need to get to the bottom of it."

"It's exactly what Loie always talked about," someone else said. "Women who resist are murdered."

"It's because she was writing a new book!"

"That's right! Where is that book? We've got to make sure it's published before they suppress it."

"Or censor it," someone else said. "The sexual liberals are always screeching about censorship, but they censor us all the time."

"They're just worried about having access to their own little sex fantasies. They don't care about the voices of real women talking about sexual abuse."

"Has anyone actually read her new book?" I put in. "Does anyone know what she was planning to say?"

There was a silence and then a woman said, almost reverently, "I believe she was planning to go much much further than she had in *The Silenced Heart*."

Several people nodded intensely.

"Further in what direction?" I persevered.

"Loie Marsh was writing her history," the woman said. "And not just her history. Our history."

"What history is that?" I inquired, but the discussion was channeled by Nan into a suggestion that a self-appointed task force see if parts of the manuscript could be read at the march.

I wasn't a meeting person and I began to lose interest as the tasks were divided. I couldn't understand it. Not one of these women seemed to see Loie as a real person, with possibly some real pain in her life that had driven her to see pornography as the thing to be fought at all costs. Loie Marsh wasn't writing history; as far as they were concerned she was history.

But it was the woman I was interested in, not the symbol. I regretted that I hadn't approached her at the conference, that I had been too awed to talk to her directly. Maybe if I had, I would have had a better idea of what kind of person she was, what motivated and possessed her.

"Now, is there someone who knows a printer who would be willing to donate the printing of the poster and flyers?" Nan asked, looking straight at me.

I nodded involuntarily. How had I managed to forget Meeting Rule Number One? Never go to a gathering of this sort unless you plan to come away on a committee.

I escaped before I could agree to anything else.

Gracie London lived in Madrona, a neighborhood of big old houses near Lake Washington. Her house was set back from the street and surrounded by tall evergreens dripping with rain. The sunny day had vanished in stormclouds during the afternoon.

We walked into a living room so filled with bookshelves that it was like looking at woven rugs, all color and pattern, lining the walls. This seemed to be Gracie's study too; a computer terminal stuck its head out of a book-and-paper-piled desk like a groundhog in spring. Next to the desk were two file cabinets and stacks of clippings and copies to be filed.

"I need a secretary," groaned Gracie. "Or to be less interested in world events. Sometimes I get my daughter to do it."

It surprised me again what an attractive woman she was. From my seat in the audience she'd looked brilliant but remote and professional. Now in the lamplight her crisp salt and pepper hair shone and her face was warm and welcoming. She was wearing black wool pants and a purple light wool shirt, with gold jewelry. She was just my height.

"So what do you want to know?" she asked me after she and June had discussed their business and we'd all had some tea. "June said she brought you along for some reason."

I didn't really lie. I said I was making some inquiries into Loie Marsh's death. Purely as a friend of Hanna's. I'd come to Gracie because I felt that she, more than most people, had a grasp of the pornography debate and the passions that fueled it.

"Oy," she said, holding out her well-shaped, capable hands, as if she wanted to fend me off. "Sometimes I wish the whole subject had never come up. Sometimes I see the history books of the twenty-first century talking about the feminist movement of the seventies and saying it disintegrated due to the pornography issue. And now you've got one of the leaders of the anti-porn movement murdered. Aside from it being a great tragedy, I can't imagine what it's going to do to the debate."

"Why do you say it's a great tragedy?" June asked. "I thought she bugged you."

"Yeah, she did! But Loie Marsh was a very gifted speaker and writer, a fantastic advocate of her ideas. And even though I increasingly opposed her, she still fascinated me. She was so *good* at her role."

I decided to jump right in and ask the question I'd hesitated to ask Pauline. "You don't think that—that Loie could have been involved in sadomasochism, do you?"

"Not in a million years—though I confess I *have* wondered what her sex life was like. She painted such disgusting pictures of adult sexuality that it was hard to imagine whether she had ever had a friendly or loving sexual connection with anyone. You get the impression from her book that she was completely obsessed with sex—she just couldn't stop talking about it, even though she had to disguise her desire to dwell on it by always describing it in the most lurid and horrific terms."

"It's true," said June. "For a woman who was so down on sex she sure had a lot to say about it."

"There's a strange voluptuousness in the writing and speaking of some of the anti-porn women. The voluptuousness of repressed desire, don't you think, Pam?"

"What? Oh yes!" For some reason I was staring at the light gold chain around her neck, at her throat. The faintly freckled skin was wrinkled a little, as if a breeze had blown over the bay and created a cobwebbed pattern on the water.

"Though the more I look at it," continued Gracie, "the more it seems like a natural development, this focus on sexuality and violence against women. In its earliest stages the feminist movement demanded recognition for women and equality. The idea was that women and men were inherently the same, with the same rights, the same abilities. From the late sixties to the mid-seventies the discussion was very much about rights—legal, economic, social. Then this new theme began to creep into the struggle. It said that women had their own biology, their own sexuality, their own history, their own ways of doing things. They weren't like men; they weren't equal to men. They were better than men. They were natural, they were in touch with their emotions, they were nurturing, spiritual, intuitive, life-enhancing and so on. In some ways this new attitude was marvelous—it took many of the qualities that women had that had been put down for centuries and suddenly not only recognized those qualities but saw them as good, as superior."

"Hey, we are superior," interrupted June. "I tell Eddy that all the time."

"It's true, we're great," said Gracie, brown eyes smiling at me, "but along with this new superior concept of womanhood came another concept that wasn't so positive—and that was the idea of woman as victim, especially victim of sexual violence. Starting in the mid-seventies came a whole spate of books, really impressive, well-researched and passionately written books that began to detail the pretty horrible things that men had been doing to women for millennia. At the time it seemed impossible not to agree with the authors—that rape, battery, incest, physical mutilation, even styles in fashion and advertising, weren't random, isolated acts performed by individual men against individual women, but a series of socially sanctioned acts designed to keep women in an oppressed position. And I still think that the recognition of the pervasiveness of violence against women by men was one of the most crucial realizations to have come out of the women's movement. Some of the institutions that women developed in response to that recognition, like rape crisis centers, self-defense workshops and the whole domestic violence network of shelters and safe houses are incredibly important contributions to the safety and well-being of women."

"You wouldn't believe that Gracie's writing a book about all this, would you?" June asked with mock-innocence. "It's called *Enough Already*."

Gracie chuckled. "I'm sorry. It's just that I've been working on the book all day and... "

"No," I said, "Go on, please. It's really interesting. What's your theory about how the split in the women's movement developed?"

"I'm sure there are lots of theories and I've held different ones at different times, but here's one possibility. First of all, the indignation and anger that developed in recognition of men's violence towards women were *reactive*, and the institutions that women developed in response were *protective*. No matter that when women got to the shelters they often went on to job training or education—the reasons that shelters were opened was specifically to protect women from violent men.

"So—and this is a little tricky—an increasingly powerful and vocal group of women activists began from the premise that if some women are raped, then all can be raped; if some women are molested, all can be molested. They formed their analysis of society around women as an oppressed class, on the basis of what has happened to some women. You don't want to say that huge numbers of women aren't raped and molested, or that we're not all *potentially* victim material, but the truth of the matter is that all women are *not* raped or molested. Yet that was proclaimed as the great unifying factor among women, rather than the fact that *most* women make far less than men and *most* women have to work much harder in lower-status jobs than men."

"It is a little contradictory," I managed to insert. I couldn't tell if I was more dazed by Gracie's flow of words or by the steady warmth of her eyes on me. June had unashamedly begun to read the front page of *The New York Times*.

"Of course all along women had been fighting this ideology of superior woman as sexual victim," Gracie went on eagerly, "whether it was proclaimed by the moral majority or the anti-pornography movement. After all, part of what had fueled the women's liberation movement in the beginning was the desire to reclaim women's sexuality. It was a desire that had passed through a number of phases, but it had never entirely gone away. It erupted again in the early eighties when women began to ask themselves and each other what had happened to exploration, experimentation and honesty when it came to sexuality. A lot of these women felt as if the anti-pornography and anti-violence against women movement had taken over sexuality and defined it as something men did, usually with evil intent, to women. Some of these women question-askers were lesbian, some heterosexual and some—horror of horrors—were a relatively new breed: lesbian sado-masochists. In reality the S/Mers were a relatively small proportion of those who were questioning the definitions, but they got a lot of attention and publicity. It suited the purposes of the anti-porn leaders to tag everyone who confessed to being interested in sexual freedom as a sado-masochist. The anti-porn women could then refer to the most extreme S/M practices as if they were common among all women who advocated freedom of sexual expression."

Gracie paused and I said the first thing that came into my mind, "Did you know that Loie—and her ex-lover Pauline—were writing a book about this same subject? It's called *We Took Back the Night*."

"Really?" said Gracie. "I'd love to get my hands on a copy. Just to see how Loie describes the period. I think we're living in a fascinating time."

"Fascinating and dangerous," June put in. "You better watch it, Gracie. You go around spouting off like this, you could be next."

Gracie looked at her sharply, then laughed. "Oh, I've always talked too much. But nobody's going to bump me off. I'm just a harmless professor."

"And Loie was a leader, is that it? Do you think that's why she was murdered? For her ideas?"

"As long as a leader is alive she has adherents," Gracie said. "She can continue to write books, to give speeches, to exert an enormous influence. Wasn't that why Stalin pursued Trotsky, why political leaders have always locked up the opposition, why other leaders have been assassinated? It's a common belief that ideas have a life of their own, that important ideas live on no matter how many people die. But the reality is that ideas are often only as strong as the person who espouses them. Kill the person, you often kill the idea."

"Well then," said June, putting down the paper and standing up to go. "You better be careful you don't have too many *ideas.*"

Gracie followed us to the door and pressed my hand as she said good-bye. "I'm just a harmless professor," she repeated.

12

"So, you liked Gracie then?" Hadley said. It was Thursday night and Hadley had met me after work at Best to suggest we go to a Japanese restaurant. Now we sat at a black lacquered table surrounded by yuppies knowledgeably ordering plates of sushi and sashimi and discussing the architectural transformation of Seattle from a provincial but original city to a clone of San Francisco. What with the building of the convention center over the freeway, the excavation under major shopping streets for the bus tunnel and the wholesale knocking down of entire blocks in order to put up new skyscrapers, the downtown center of Seattle had become a sort of black hole. A favorite topic of conversation these days consisted of wondering what the city would look like when it was all over, whether in fact we could still be said to be living in Seattle. An interesting metaphysical conceit, I thought, though the yuppies weren't doing it justice.

"Oh yes," I said, spearing a piece of tempura sweet potato, "She was very—stimulating."

Hadley nodded and finished off the shrimp. "Remember last week you said you'd be willing to talk about living situations this week?"

"Oh dear, is this the day?"

"Well, have you been thinking about it?"

"Yes. I've decided to move to New Zealand."

"What?"

"Just kidding. No, I haven't thought about it. I've had too much else to think about."

"You know, Penny and Ray are ready to buy you out of that house whenever you want. You could use the money to make a down payment on something else."

"On a house for myself? And what would you do—buy a house for yourself?"

"The market's good right now."

"Hadley—you've been looking for a *house*?" Without thinking I swallowed a too-large bit of wasabi, straight, and my throat burned with the fire of the horseradish paste.

"My eye sometimes wanders through the real estate ads," she admitted.

"Couldn't we live together in your house then? You could get a big one. Four stories—twenty rooms? We could each have a wing and meet for dinner twice a week?"

"Oh Pam," she said, smiling. "This isn't easy."

"What are you so afraid of anyway," I asked. "Aside from you bumping your head on the ceiling we seem to be doing okay living together. We both like the same foods, we're both relatively neat and considerate. Yet we have separate interests and friends. We're the model couple really. What would be so awful and different if we made it permanent?"

"That's just it." Hadley's blue-green eyes darkened as she fastened on this word. "Permanency. Routine. The death of spontaneity. Lesbian marriage. The end of being able to come and go freely. The end of adventure. Entropy."

"I get the picture," I said. "But just when are you so into spontaneity and coming and going? You came back to Seattle partly to be with me and now you're running this business which takes all your time. Where do you think you're going? Living together isn't death. It's just saying to the world that we're a couple, that we choose each other."

"I don't want to say anything to the world," said Hadley. "I'm only interested in talking to you."

That was my sore point, that I did care what people thought of me. I did want to make a statement to the world—and maybe to my sister most of all—that I was part of a successful couple, just a normal person, really, in spite of being a lesbian. To show I didn't mind, I said, "Oh well, no big deal. I'll start asking around to see if anyone knows of a place. . . . "

I said it a little pathetically, if the truth be told, to give Hadley a chance to reconsider, but she just nodded and downed the last of her tea. "Yes, both of us need to be looking now."

We left the restaurant and started walking through the International District, crowded with people doing their shopping and going out for dinner. The evening was a clear black one, with a snap in the air, and all of a sudden I didn't feel too bad. We had our lives before us, it was probably better not to rush into things, and besides, it wasn't as if Hadley had said anything about *leaving* me.

"Since we're in the neighborhood," she said casually, "and it's Thursday night, why don't we stop by Miko's to see her videos? There's sure to be a crowd of people there who were at the conference. Maybe you could learn something."

"Maybe I could," I said, trying to keep my fists from balling up in the pockets of my jacket and the suspicion out of my mind that Hadley had engineered our tempura in order to put us in the neighborhood. "I really would love to pin something on Miko."

Miko lived and worked in an upstairs studio off Jackson Street, above a Chinese herbalist whose windows were full of mysterious black roots and fungi. The door to her place wasn't easy to find; it was in an alley and hidden by piles of used boxes with Chinese words stenciled on them. When we finally arrived, the videos had already begun. The room was dark and it was impossible to see exactly who was there. I thought there might be ten or twelve women. Hadley and I stood in back, peering at a not very big TV screen placed on a table. The sound of panting filled the room suddenly; it wasn't coming from any of the audience, nor from the two figures on the screen who were, I could see now, sitting rather demurely across from each other at a kitchen table.

Their mouths opened and closed silently—they seemed to be having an ordinary chat about work or relationships—while the background noise of panting grew louder and louder. Suddenly one of the women, dark-haired and rather sullen, reached across the narrow table and slowly lifted up the other woman's sweater. The second woman was a peroxide blonde and wore a black lace bra. The panting went on, a little more subdued. The camera focused for an inordinate amount of time on the woman's breasts, which were quite large and soft. First one breast, then the other. The panting noises began to build again; unconsciously the audience pressed forward slightly. Still in close-up, a hand pulled one of the black lace cups away from the breast; an enormous nipple slipped out. Long fingers caressed it to a state of erectness. Then the same thing happened with the other nipple. The panting rose and fell and as it rose and fell a pair of lips fastened themselves on the nipple. The breast filled the screen behind the dark head like the backdrop for a surrealistic play.

And so it went, predictable, though not any the less suspenseful for that. The panting rose and fell, and when it fell a new part of the body was revealed for the dark-haired woman to set upon. The women's faces never came into focus again, nor were there any words exchanged between them. The video ended with a long shot of a glistening clitoris, while the panting ebbed and died.

The second video had slightly more of a plot. Two women were walking along through a woods. Occasionally sunlight dappled their faces; they were talking, but the voice-over seemed to suggest that the inner thoughts were quite different from what was being said aloud.

"... her thighs... It would ruin everything."

"I might have to deal with the consequences."

"Maybe Joyce would understand... monogamy is such an outdated concept after all... "

"If only I could... touch her.... "

"I want it so much I could.... "

They went on like this for about five minutes. Obviously the audience expected them to throw caution, monogamy and commitment to the wind and get it on right there in the forest, because when they didn't, when they merely parted with kisses on the cheek and rather rueful smiles, the women in the room erupted with surprise and derision.

"Call that a sex video?" someone muttered.

The third video was longer than the others. Miko said it was called "Homage to Luce Irigaray," adding even more obscurely and helpfully for those of us who didn't know who or what she was talking about, "The Sex Which Is Not One."

The text, such as it was, consisted of the words repeated, in various voices and in various tones: *Women have sex organs more or less everywhere.* This rather alarming idea was illustrated by close-ups of parts of many different women's bodies. It was very lovingly photographed: shots of an elbow bending so forearm and upper arm met were juxtaposed with shots of vaginal lips parting and coming together again. It reminded me a little of Edward Weston's photography. Still I couldn't help agreeing after ten minutes with a woman nearby who groaned, scarcely under her breath, "Bor-ing."

To tell the truth, I hadn't expected Miko's videos to be quite so, well, artistic. I had been imagining lesbian orgies and sex romps—not adventures into the meaning of sexuality for women. I was apparently not the only one, because when the lights came up and Miko, wearing a flame-red stretch jumpsuit, said, a little anxiously, "Does anyone want to discuss these?" there was an immediate chorus of, "That wasn't sexy!"

Hadley grinned at me and whispered, "I think they were expecting *Dyke Does Dallas.*"

I laughed and looked around to see if I recognized anyone and saw Nicky in a black crepe dress and Oak in full leather down in front, among Miko's loudest detractors.

"We wanted to see real pornography," Oak complained.

Miko was standing up bravely to the onslaught. "So what wasn't sexy about them?"

"Too much talking."

"Not enough talking."

Miko held out perplexed hands. "Which?"

"Not enough *sexy* talking."

"So we've got a distinction between sexy talking and talking about sex," said Miko. "Can somebody give me an example of sexy talking?"

"Sexy talking is *You want me to lick your pussy, cunt? Then beg me for it,*" said Oak.

"Yeah!" shouted someone. Others hissed.

"I found the inner dialog in the second video extremely sexy," said a woman with a burgundy ponytail and harlequin glasses. "The sexual tension between the two women was elaborated by the use of language, which, tentative and fragile though it was, nevertheless served to highlight the ironic structure of the exchange."

"Well, I think it was just a cunt tease," said Oak.

"Yes, but on whose part?" a woman all in gray said reasonably. "I think Miko was doing something very subtle, especially at the end when the two women walked off. In a certain sense you could say that the women *did* have a sexual exchange. In every way except the physical they were unfaithful to their partners."

"In every way except the physical!" Nicky burst out. "You make it sound as if we're living in Victorian times, when women could apparently get off just by writing twenty-page letters to their best friends. Sex in the eighties is about the physical. Yes, the physical! Finally!"

"Not necessarily," said the woman in gray. "For a lot of people in the eighties physical sex is about fear and disease and death. A great deal of it is going to take place in the mind from now on."

"Well, I liked the first one best," someone interrupted. "After a while the panting got a little irritating, but I really liked the suspense before each part of the woman's body was revealed. To me that's what the erotic impulse is about—fantasizing about the unknown. So I think tension and suspense are a really important part of lesbian erotica and I thought you did it really well, Miko."

"Thank you," Miko said gratefully.

"Do you think of your work as lesbian erotica or as pornography?" Hadley asked.

"Are you kidding?" said Oak. "What we just watched is *not* pornography."

Miko said, "I don't really know how to define pornography. If the point of pornography is only to stimulate the genitals, then I'd have to say no, I don't make pornography. Yet clearly, I am thinking of turning my audience on—but it's more in order to make them think about what's turning them on and how. I'm against the term erotica, because I don't think it means anything different from pornography. It has connotations of soft-focusing and upper-class pretensions, but it's really the same thing. And as a lesbian video maker *all* my work is considered pornographic and subject to censorship."

Then a brave person asked who Luce Irigaray was, anyway, and the discussion veered off into pre-linguistic erotic energy, anti-phallocentric language and the morphology of the female body. Even Hadley suddenly started talking about Lacan and Nicky came up with some interesting observations about modernism as a hidden language for Djuna Barnes and Gertrude Stein. Only two of us remained silent: me, because I was somewhat out of my depth (the last philosophical work I'd read had been Hobbes's *Leviathan* in graduate school), and Oak, who was sitting, angry and withdrawn, exuding clouds of disappointment. I found her a little frightening, to tell the truth. I wasn't sure what sadists did, but with forearms like those it didn't seem like you were likely to get off easy.

Finally the discussion showed signs of sputtering out in semiotic doubletalk, and people began to make their way out of the studio.

Miko came up to Hadley and me and thanked us profusely for coming.

"Wow, Hadley," she enthused. "I never realized you were such an intellectual. You can shoot the structuralist shit with the best of them."

"I had a lot of free time last winter," Hadley said, and took my hand.

For an instance I almost felt like jerking my fingers out of hers, to punish her for even being friendly to Miko in my presence, but fortunately it passed. I wasn't sure why, but Hadley wasn't responding to Miko the way she had been. I'd be a fool if I took it that way.

"I thought the videos were interesting, Miko," I said.

She turned teasingly to me, "But did you find them sexy?"

"Intellectually sexy, maybe."

"Good!" she said. "I always say, the way to a woman's body is through her head." She turned away to flirt with someone else and Hadley and I began to walk towards the door. We ran into Nicky and Oak, who looked as if they were in serious discussion.

"Do you have a minute, Nicky?" I suddenly asked.

"No," Oak said. "What do you want?"

"I just have a couple of questions." I didn't pause to ask if she'd answer them, but went on, "You said you used to know Hanna and Loie. When was that?"

Nicky looked bored. "I don't remember. Years ago."

"But when?"

"I'm telling you, I can't remember. They weren't close friends."

"But you said Hanna and Loie hadn't spoken to you for years—that made it sound as if... "

Oak had her by the arm and was almost jerking her away from me. "If we're going to do it, let's, Nicky— come on."

Nicky gave me a curious, but detached look. "Well, I hadn't had contact with them recently. So if that's all... "

"Just one last thing." I began to follow them in the direction of Miko. "What was Loie's husband's name? I know it was David. David what?"

"David Gustafson," Nicky said.

I stopped following them. "Not the Christian... "

"The very same," Nicky called back with what sounded like a chortle. "The very same."

"This gets more and more interesting," I told Hadley on the way home. "Loie married to Sonya Gustafson's husband. Mrs. Christians Against Pornography. And they were going to be on the same panel."

"They were," agreed Hadley.

"What do you mean?"

"Just what I said. They were."

13

I DECIDED THAT I WANTED to meet Mr. and Mrs. Gustafson, but I couldn't figure out what excuse I should use. After work on Friday I went to the downtown library and looked through microfiches of *The Seattle Times* for references to them and their group. There were quite a few. I also found out that David had written a small pamphlet called *Strategies Against Smut*. Thus armed I gave them a call Saturday afternoon to say I was a housewife who volunteered for a small Christian newsletter in Southern California—Orange County. I was just up in Seattle to visit a friend and I'd heard of their fine work against pornography and wondered if they would consent to being interviewed for the newsletter.

They would consent. With pleasure. On Sunday afternoon, after church.

I went over to my sister's Saturday evening to ransack her closet for something to wear to the interview. Unlike me, Penny had kept clothes from all stages of her life and there was always something useful somewhere in her wardrobe.

I found her and Ray at home, spending the evening in, with the VCR and Antonia.

"This isn't like you two," I said. "Don't you have a benefit for Central America to go to? A mailing? A meeting? What's happened to my two favorite politicos on the go?"

"It's harder to haul around a baby than you might imagine," said Penny, somewhat defensively. She had already changed into her bathrobe, and so had Ray. Both of them looked about ten years older than they had yesterday at the print shop. "They cry at the wrong times, they need to have their diapers changed. . . It always used to look like fun—babies in backpacks—but it seems to be a lot of work."

"We took Toni over to some friends last night for dinner," said Ray. "And she was fussy and kept crying the whole time. You can't have a reasonable conversation when that's happening. We had to leave right after the meal, and then she kept us up all night."

"This morning she was fine. She was fine until I tried to take a nap, in fact," said Penny blearily. "Then she screamed non-stop for two hours. It's like torture. It really is."

"Look at her," said Ray, gesturing to the little angel a-sleep on the couch next to him. "Out like a light, but at one o'clock this morning I bet she starts in again."

Her parents looked at my niece as if she were a bomb wrapped up in tissue paper.

"You should let me baby-sit for you sometime," I offered. As the words came out of my mouth I realized it was the first time in Antonia's short life that I'd mentioned taking her. I added hesitantly, "for a few hours sometime or something."

I suppose I expected Penny to snap, "You—take care of *my* baby! What if something happened??" But instead she said, quite gratefully, "Oh, would you sometime, Pam? That would be great."

*

The Gustafsons lived on an unremarkable street in a middle-class area of Bellevue, the city across Lake Washington that had grown from a suburb of Seattle to something mysteriously large, with skyscrapers, shopping malls and an identity crisis.

I smoothed down my skirt and jacket nervously after I rang the bell and hoped they wouldn't think my black tights were too bohemian. Still, it was better than hairy legs.

When Sonya opened the door and invited me inside her attractive home, I felt as if my television set had sprung a door and let me into a commercial for a furniture showroom. Everything was good quality; nothing was original. It was strange how you relied on people's tacky and/or idiosyncratic tastes in decorating to give you a sense of their personality. This house had no such items; it could have been rented.

Sonya was a little like that too. Although she hadn't been able to construct her own body, she made the most of what she had. She was, in a rather spectacular way, what used to be called in home economics classes "well-groomed."

"Remember the little things—they're what make the difference," our teacher used to say (while some of us reprobates snorted). Sonya remembered the little things. Her blue pumps were the exact shade of her dress; the gold and blue scarf at her neck picked up the gold of her button earrings. Her nails were manicured and their polish matched her lipstick. Noticing the perfection of the little things made it harder to see the larger picture—which was that Sonya was actually somewhat ugly, with a large nose, heavy jaw and eyes set close together. But what was ugliness anyway? My home ec teacher would have said that no girl can be unattractive if she is well-groomed.

I felt every hair on my legs straining to get through the black tights.

Sonya graciously led me into the living room, where David Gustafson was waiting, then she vanished to the kitchen for coffee.

"No trouble finding the place, I hope, Randy?" David said kindly.

"Oh no... Thank you."

I think I'd been expecting him to be booming and charismatic, like Jimmy Swaggert or Pat Robertson. But his manner was almost gentle as he waited for me to sit down and sat down himself. He was on the short side, neat and compact in a suit and tie. His sandy hair was thinning; he still had boyish freckles and a lovable smile.

His voice felt like a handshake, pumping me up and down. How was I enjoying Seattle? Who was my friend and what was her church? What was my church down in California and what was the newsletter called?

I was sweating slightly by the time Sonya came back in. Before she could begin to ask me questions too, I took the enthusiastic offensive.

"I've heard so much about what you've done up here to wipe out smut and I really would like to hear all about it. Pornography is such a problem where I come from."

"Yes, we've had real success here," said Sonya. "Thank God times are changing. Part of it is AIDS and people at last beginning to understand that you reap what you sow, and part of it is the work that Christians have been doing. People seem to be turning away from the worst forms of pornography."

"How long have you been involved in the struggle?" I asked, wondering if struggle was the right word. That's what they said on the left; maybe Christians had another word for it—Christian endeavor?

David and Sonya looked at each other, and David took Sonya's hand. He said, "I think it started when Sonya came home from the drug store one day some years back. She'd just been ignoring the magazines as usual, but on this occasion, our six-year-old daughter had got hold of a copy of *Oui* magazine and she asked Sonya what the lady was doing... "

"I don't know what came over me," Sonya continued.

"I'd always been kind of a quiet person, very shy. If they didn't fix the car right at the garage I never complained, and if the soup was too cold in a restaurant I always thought, well, I won't tell the waiter, it's too embarrassing and maybe he's having a bad evening, and anyway, it's not *that* cold. But when Dede held up that copy of *Oui* I saw red. I marched up to the counter and I said to the clerk, in a very loud voice, 'Sir, since when is it the practice of your store to display pictures like this so that any child walking by can see them?' And I opened the magazine and held up a photograph of a woman tied at the wrists to a bedpost, being beaten—artistically, of course. When they want to make something artistic they make the scene Edwardian.

"Everyone was shocked, especially the clerk. He started to mumble something about not knowing what was in the magazines, the wholesalers just came and filled up the racks. But I said that I wasn't going to be palmed off with excuses, that I wasn't going to rest until every porn magazine was removed from the shelves. And do you know what? The other women in line cheered!

"A week later, after organizing a letter campaign to the store's manager and a boycott of the store, the porn magazines were off the shelves."

"And that's where it all started," said David. "As Christians, we felt the best way we could demonstrate our faith would be to work against the sale and distribution of smut. We always say, 'If every Christian, every time he or she went into a store that carries porn, complained and caused a fuss, then porn would disappear in a few weeks.'"

I murmured my admiration, and wrote it down while thinking that Sonya showed a grasp of direct action techniques that any anarchist could admire.

"David has concentrated more on the legal aspect of things," said Sonya. "Trying to get existing obscenity laws enforced, working for new legislation, while I've done more community organizing, boycotts and fundraising."

"'Direct action is no substitute for work in the courts and halls of government,'" David quoted. "Martin Luther

King."

Well, he wouldn't be the first conservative to have started out in civil rights or the student movement. Student movement—I wonder if this might be a possible lead-in to Loie and how they met. . .

"Most people," said David, "don't realize that there are laws on the books already about pornography. We've gotten so used to seeing the spread of smut since the seventies into our neighborhoods, libraries and stores that we think it's legal. That we can't do anything about it."

Sonya added, "A lot of people have a problem with the definition of obscene. That's where the ACLU and a lot of liberals have gotten tangled up."

"How do you define obscene then?" I asked, pen poised.

David had it on the tip of his tongue. "Any matter or performance is obscene if 1) The average person, applying contemporary community standards, finds that the matter or performance, taken as a whole, appeals to the prurient interest, and 2) the matter or performance depicts or describes, in a patently offensive way, sexual conduct, normal or perverted, actual or simulated, and 3) the matter or performance, taken as a whole, lacks serious literary, artistic, political or scientific value."

I smiled brightly. "Average person? Community standards? Don't those vary?"

"Not really," said David confidently. "Statistics show that eighty percent of Americans oppose pornography. We have to assume then that it's still around because there is a small percentage of sex addicts encouraged by an atmosphere of decadence and supported by rich pornographers and their lawyers. But we believe that pornography is only present in a community if citizens allow it. Once decent people become aware of its pervasive filth and realize that they can fight it, pornography disappears."

"Of course there will always be sexual perversion," said Sonya. "But at least we don't have sadomasochism, homosexuality and other forms of bestiality shoved down our throats in public and displayed openly to our children."

Homosexuality and other forms of bestiality? I began to sweat a little more violently in my jacket.

But David had gotten back to M.L. King. "We can't make people love what is right," he said earnestly. "But we can make them *obey* what is right. That's what laws are for. It's just like you can't end racism legally. You can't make whites care about black people, and love them as their sisters and brothers. But you *can* make them obey civil rights laws."

"That sounds like what Andrea Dworkin and Catherine MacKinnon have been saying, when they drafted the ordinance in Minneapolis."

"That's right," said Sonya. "We support that ordinance; we'd like to get one like it passed here."

"You must have known Loie Marsh then?" I rushed on. Time was getting short and I wanted to get out of here. "The woman who was killed in Seattle last week?"

"Well," said David, apparently at a loss. But Sonya carried on smoothly, "She and I were scheduled to be on a panel that evening, the evening she was... unfortunately... "

"I just thought maybe you knew her. Your ideas are similar, about pornography... aren't they?"

David's sweet face had been darkening through my artless speech.

"A woman who was a known—a flagrant—homosexual had no business lecturing other people about smut."

"Oh, my goodness!" I said, trying to look shocked. "Loie Marsh. Why, I believed—I think someone told me—she was married. Yes, I'm sure of it."

"Davey," said Sonya. "I'm sure Randy could use another cup of coffee and this pot is cold. *Could* you? Thanks, sweetie."

When he was out of the room she hurriedly turned to me and said, "I'm afraid Loie Marsh is rather a sore subject for my husband. You see, when he was quite young, in college, he made a mistake. The fact of the matter is... you see, he was married to Loie for a brief time. It was quite a miserable time for him. She was older and rather... fast. I believe even then that she had sinful leanings and that she tempted him on several occasions."

"Oh my goodness," I said again, though I was dying to ask what the sinful leanings and temptations had consisted of.

"Yes," Sonya seemed thoughtful, "considering Loie's past, it's a mystery to me how she ever got involved in the anti-pornography movement. I would have liked to have given her the benefit of the doubt and considered her an ally, in spite of her homosexuality—I've always thought that it was important to make coalitions with the anti-pornography feminists, after all we really want the same thing— but David was always adamant that we have nothing to do with her. And since she died the way she did, I guess he was right."

I wanted to say that being murdered wasn't exactly an expression of personality, but instead I asked, "So he never saw her again—after they got divorced?"

"Not as long as we've been together, which has been fifteen years. He doesn't like to talk about her—he feels very bitter."

I shook my head, as if I were wondering at the strangeness of the world, and tried one last question, "Isn't it funny about college romances. I remember one boyfriend I had who turned out to be a member of the Communist Party." (That was true, actually, but at the time I thought it more romantic than reprehensible.) "However did they meet?"

Sonya smiled and gently stroked the pillow beside her. "David was quite the budding actor once. I believe he met Loie because he knew her cousin through acting classes. Or maybe it was Hanna's roommate, Nicky. I knew them slightly too. Even then Hanna Sandbakker was quite a fine actress."

"Did you say Nicky?"

"Yes. Why?" said Sonya, giving me a sharp look.

I fumbled. "It's just that Nicky is my son's name... and for a moment I thought... silly of me... co-ed education didn't go quite that far...." I gave a little laugh to show I was just a pleasant sort of nitwit and Sonya relaxed.

David returned with fresh coffee and a calmer demeanor. We spent another five minutes discussing Seattle and Bellevue and then I took my leave.

That evening Hadley and I had dinner with Moe and Allen at their place. The four of us had gotten together a few times over the summer, mainly for a movie and coffee afterwards. This was the first time we'd been over to their apartment, which was small but spectacularly situated on the western side of Queen Anne Hill. We sipped glasses of lemon-flavored Calistoga while we watched a hot mango sun slip down behind the sharply etched slate gray of the Olympics.

Allen looked better than I'd seen him looking in some time. His face had filled out and his eyes were beginning to lose that haunted quality that had been so apparent when he first moved to Seattle in July. He talked animatedly about a new job he'd just gotten, as a waiter for a small new lakeside restaurant in the Leschi neighborhood. "It's been fabulous to get out among people again," he said. "It's just done me so much good. And since I only work four nights a week, Moe and I still have a lot of time together."

Moe gave him an affectionate look. "It's fun to see you dressed up with a bow tie again. It's a very fancy restaurant—and the leftovers are great!"

Allen had prepared one of the recipes from the restaurant for us—chicken in a puree of raspberries and crème fraîche, braised fennel and a salad of warm wild rice and vegetables. We ate appreciatively and talked about everything except the bus tunnel. Gradually the conversation swung around to Loie and her violent death.

"It's been a week since it happened," said Moe, push-ing his plate away and patting his slightly rounded stomach. "You'd think they'd have found some clue."

"Maybe they have," I said. "Maybe they're working away at it right now, infiltrating the local S/M community with trained personnel. Maybe right this minute Officer Mary Catherine O'Malley has got someone in her clutches and is torturing her to get at the truth. Strangling her with rosary beads or something."

"Who do you think did it?" asked Allen.

I shook my head and returned to finishing my salad. Pauline was the obvious choice if it weren't for the log-istics. But I'd picked up so many funny vibrations from others, among them Elizabeth Ketteridge, David Gustaf-son, Nicky Kay. I had the feeling all of them knew things about Loie Marsh and her past that they weren't, for vari-ous reasons, terribly eager to share. I thought of Mrs. Sandbakker's cryptic comment about Loie maybe having deserved it, and Hanna's outburst when reminded by her mother that Loie had saved her life. I still thought from time to time of the therapist who'd once been into S/M. If I thought about it, I could be suspicious of everyone I'd met, even of Gracie London claiming she was just a harm-less professor.

But it wasn't my job to be suspicious. I was just curious, that's all. Sometimes I thought it all had to do with my parents, this odd need to pursue the causes of people's deaths. If I could find a reason for a murder, maybe there was a reason for an accidental death as well. Following a line of investigation was an active response anyway. You didn't just sit there, stunned with sorrow, you asked questions, you demanded answers, you looked for motives, causes, a pattern.

And sometimes there *were* answers, sometimes there *were* causes, sometimes there *was* a pattern. My curiosity was justified, my grief, temporarily, assuaged.

"I really don't understand this obsession in the feminist movement with pornography," Allen was saying. "There's

125

been porn in the gay community for years and it hasn't hurt us. Most of us grew up on it, it was the only way we had of forming a positive response to our sexuality."

"Maybe if there'd been lesbian porn—produced by lesbians for lesbians—when we were growing up then we'd have a different response to porn too," said Hadley tartly.

"Then where did you get your information about sex when you were growing up?" Moe was curious.

"I got all mine from my sister and the girl down the block," I said. "But it *wasn't* about lesbian sex, it was all girl-boy stuff. I guess I gradually became aware through some books I read, Colette, de Beauvoir, that there were lesbians. It was definitely connected with France for a while."

"My information came through books too," said Hadley. "But they were a little more pulpy. Sarah Aldridge. Ann Bannon. Isabel Miller. A girl in high school turned me on to them. And then we all read *The Well of Loneliness* and *The Group* in college. And some people read Djuna Barnes and Gertrude Stein, but it was hard to find anything particularly sexy in them."

"So you never masturbated to pictures of naked women?" Allen pressed.

"Never," I said.

"Well," Hadley said. "A few times. It meant getting a copy of *Playboy* and then trying to hide it."

Moe nodded. "So much of gay sex in the seventies when I came out seemed to be in direct response to the repression we'd all suffered as boys. You had thousands of gay men flooding into San Francisco, ready to act out things we'd only dreamed of. Porn was part of that, but it always seemed to me that porn was something you did when you couldn't get sex. I spent weekend nights when my parents were out with a whole stack of male porn magazines when I was in high school. It felt so shameful. I even did it on Shabbes. But when I came to San Francisco the shame was over. There was this feeling of immense sexual joy. . . . "

"That's all gone now," said Allen, picking at his chicken bones. "I suppose porn has come back more strongly to compensate."

"There was never that sexual joy in the lesbian-feminist community," said Hadley a little enviously. "Casual sex was frowned on, the idea of tricking was morally repugnant. Monogamy, even if it had to be serial, was the way to go."

"But you've been together eight years or something," I said to Allen and Moe. "So you're a good example of a committed gay relationship."

"Sure we are," said Moe. "But we've never insisted on sexual fidelity either. We probably both fucked dozens of men, but that had no effect on our commitment."

I tried to think how I'd feel if Hadley were out every night making love with other women. I just couldn't imagine it working. But was that because of my repressed nature or because we'd never tried it or because women had a different history and a different set of expectations?

"Sex for lesbians is totally tied up in relationships," said Hadley. "We don't have a way of getting erotic needs met outside the relationship—unless we have an affair, which is another relationship."

Was she saying that she had erotic needs I wasn't meeting? Was she saying she was having an affair? She suddenly looked incredibly desirable to me across the table, in her red sweater, with round red earrings, her silvery hair tucked behind her ears.

"A lot of lesbians," Allen said a little morosely, "haven't been able to support gay men during the AIDS crisis because somehow they feel like gay men are being paid back for all that screwing around."

"I remember when the AIDS epidemic first began," said Hadley. "A lot of lesbians were very smug. It was as if those years of serial monogamy had paid off. Now they were being rewarded by keeping their health."

"Be fair," said Moe. "If it had only been lesbians who were getting sick there would have been even less of an outcry and far fewer resources, if only because so few women have money."

I thought back to when I'd first heard of AIDS. I hadn't been a lesbian then and I'd absorbed the news rather indifferently. It was just some kind of virus gay men who went to bathhouses in San Francisco got, kind of like Legionnaire's Disease.

"I think lesbians have changed their attitude," said Hadley. "The losses have been too great for anybody to ignore them."

We were all silent.

"Oh dear," said Allen, with forced cheerfulness. "Funny how that subject *does* have a way of rearing its ugly head."

"It's the question of the century," said Moe. "Now that we know there's sex without procreation, can we believe there's sex without consequences?"

"Or sex without oppression?" I added.

"Or sex without chocolate?" Hadley asked, bringing out her surprise, half a Chocolate Decadence cake from the Dilettante cafe.

It was on the way home from Allen and Moe's that we heard the news. In the midst of the radio babble, as Hadley was changing stations searching for her favorite song (Hadley was the kind of girl who still had favorite songs), it was announced that a woman had been found strangled this evening in Seattle.

His voice salivating so that we would realize that this was no ordinary, run-of-the-mill murder of a woman, the announcer said, "She was a Ph.D. candidate—and an exotic dancer at the Fun Palace."

14

THE LOCAL NEWS MEDIA had had kept a wary distance from Loie Marsh. Whatever the unsavory details of her death, much of her public life had been spent fighting violence against women, and in Seattle, at least, that was something to respect. Possibly more to the point, her family was obviously good, decent Scandinavian stock. Soon, no doubt, a reporter was bound to pick up some of the things I'd learned and use them in a profile that would smear her memory while pretending to be sympathetic, but so far it hadn't happened.

Nicky Kay's murder didn't get the kid glove treatment. The papers interviewed her professors at Stanford; the TV cameras focused on the exterior of the Fun Palace. Even Djuna Barnes, *Nightwood* and the twenties in Paris were thrown into the story. It was everything that the media loves. "The Double Life of Nicky Kay." "Student's Secret Life." In reality there had been nothing secret or double about Nicky's life. She'd been one of the more upfront people I'd ever met in my life.

On the other hand the media helped me piece a few things together. From the two papers and the local TV station I found out that Nicky had been a brilliant student at the University of Washington, had gone to Stanford first for a Masters, then a Ph.D. in English. She had apparently worked in a strip joint in the North Beach. Three years ago she'd returned to Seattle to work on her thesis. Her advisors and professors were uniformly "shocked."

All in all they managed to dig up lots of dirt on Nicky as a sex worker. But further than that they didn't go. Either the mention of sadomasochism was unthinkable for family TV and newspapers, or they didn't have a clue. If they'd wanted they could have splashed the papers with lurid accounts of Nicky's speech at the conference and hinted at all sorts of rude and nasty goings-on, but there was no reference anywhere to Nicky's sexual preference or predilections or to her relationship with Oak. And though they said Nicky had been strangled, the media didn't link her murder with Loie's. Did that mean Nicky hadn't been found with a dog collar around her neck?

Or did it mean that the police were keeping that bit of information to themselves?

I decided to call up the one person I knew who was even remotely connected to the world of journalism, an old political cohort who had once worked on the alternative, now defunct, *Northwest Passage*. Sandy had recently become the Washington State governor's press secretary.

As I expected, she wasn't particularly delighted to hear from me. For the last couple of years she'd been trying to put some distance between her and her more radical past.

"No Pam, I am not going to call up my 'reporter friends' and ask them what 'implement' was used to strangle this exotic dancer."

"But Sandy, the newspapers aren't saying and I can hardly call up the police department and ask them myself."

"Pam, I can't abuse my position." She was patient. "Do you know how many people are constantly trying to worm information out of me about the governor's policies? This is a good job and I don't want to lose it."

"This isn't to do with the toxic waste bill, hon. It's just a simple murder case. For old time's sake? Remember Satsop?"

I was pulling on her heartstrings. We had once been in the same affinity group that had gotten lost in the woods attempting to occupy the site where the Satsop nuclear power plants were to be built. By the time Sandy and I and a woman named Colleen had finally staggered onto the site it was twilight and everybody else had already been arrested. We almost had to beg the sheriff to take us in too, just so we could be sure we'd get home before dark. It's ignominious moments like that that either destroy or eternally bind friendships.

But Sandy wasn't moved. "Colleen tried that one on me last month," she said crisply, "Wanting to know if the governor was going to support the low-income housing bill."

"Oh well," I sighed. "Maybe when I have something really important to ask you. . . . "

A half hour later she called me back. "Nicky Kay was strangled by a thin cord of some sort, probably leather or plastic," she said with some repugnance. "She wasn't choked by the dog collar that was found around her neck. The detectives think that the same person also may have murdered Loie Marsh, but they asked the media not to reveal the m.o. yet for fear of copycat murders. That what you wanted to know?"

"Sandy, you're a pal."

She laughed. "We did have a good time back then, didn't we?"

Penny didn't come into work on Monday. She called from Group Health to say Toni had an ear infection, that that's why she'd been screaming. It wasn't serious and had already started to clear up. Ray came in but he was so tired from being up all night that he spent most of the morning lying on the office couch. Moe, June and I finally got tired of tiptoeing around him and made him go home.

"They're too old to have kids," June clucked. "That's

the problem."

"What do you mean, June?" Moe asked. "They're only thirty or so, aren't they?"

"You want to have all that baby stuff over by the time you're twenty," June said sagely. "My girls'll be out of the house before I'm forty. Then I'm going to live."

Around mid-afternoon Hanna called, asking for Penny and sounding very worked up.

I assumed she was upset to have heard about Nicky. After all, they had been college roommates. But Nicky seemed to be the furthest thing from her mind.

"Loie's manuscript has been stolen!"

"What? The new book she was working on? How do you know?"

"A detective came over this morning asking to look through her papers again. I thought everything was in a couple of boxes, but when I pulled them out, one of the boxes was half empty."

"How do you know that's where Loie kept it? Had you ever seen the manuscript before?"

"Of course I'd seen the manuscript," said Hanna. "She completely took over my study with her papers. She had two file boxes for the project. One labeled *We Took Back the Night* and the other one *Notes*. And now the manuscript and half the notes are gone."

"Who do you think could have taken them?"

"I don't know. But I've got to get them back!"

"Why? Now that Loie's dead the book will never be finished. It will never be published, will it?"

With an effort Hanna took control of herself and said, "No, that's right. It won't be published. I suppose I'm more upset that someone's been in the house. Whoever murdered Loie wanted that manuscript—and they broke into my house to get it."

"I'd be upset too," I said, and I told her to call Penny at home.

By the time we said good-bye Hanna was composed again. I wondered if, as an actress, she had learned to calculate the effectiveness of her outbursts, or whether they came upon her unawares, and uncontrollably.

The Espressomat was not its usual lively self that evening. In spite of the steady hum of steaming machines, there was a kind of stillness at the heart of it. It had only been a couple of weeks since I'd sat here wondering whether I should go to the conference. What had been mildly intriguing and provocative had turned sour. There was someone in Seattle who was sick with fear or revenge, someone who had needed to make sure Loie couldn't speak on the panel that evening. Someone who for some reason had also needed to kill Nicky. According to what Sandy had told me it was the same person, but what was the link?

If Loie had been involved in sadomasochism there might have been a reason to kill her. It wasn't absolutely impossible. Look at the TV evangelists. The more they talked about the evils of leading an immoral life, the more they ranted against pornography and prostitution and homosexuality, the more they secretly felt compelled to act out their fantasies and engage in extramarital fornication. Jimmy Swaggert said he'd been fascinated by pornography since he was a boy. Being an ultra-right-wing Christian fundamentalist had been both a cover and a prop for him. He may have struggled against his tendencies only to be drawn irrevocably back to them. Perhaps Loie had too. Perhaps she and Nicky had been lovers years ago when they were both students. Maybe they'd taken up again when Loie returned to Seattle. And Oak had found out. . . .

It was difficult to keep Oak out of my mind. She was big and she was a proclaimed sadist. Those great forearms would have no trouble tightening a dog collar or a leash around someone's throat. But even if Oak had killed Loie and Nicky in a vengeful love triangle, why would she have stolen the manuscript? It didn't make sense.

Hadley took a break and came over. "I should be ready

to go soon," she said apologetically. "Amanda went home sick today. Why didn't anyone ever tell me that being an employer was a little like being a school nurse?"

I asked her sympathetically if I could bring her a cup of coffee or something, and she vaguely shuddered. "An orange juice would be nice," she said. "Thanks honey."

While I was up at the counter getting it for her I saw Miko come in. She was far from her flamboyant self. Instead she slipped in like an animal looking for shelter.

"Hi Pam," she said in a flat subdued voice.

"Hi." It was strange to see Miko looking so vulnerable. "Come and sit down with us if you want, after you've got your coffee."

She looked almost pathetically grateful. What was with her? Surely it couldn't be Nicky's murder? She'd hardly known Nicky.

Hadley picked up on it too. "How's life in videoland these days?"

Miko shrugged. "All right."

"I thought that evening at your studio last week was really interesting," I volunteered, with a vague feeling I was repeating myself. To my horror Miko's eyes began to fill with tears. She wasn't the crying type—somehow that made it worse.

The Espressomat's remaining employee, Lillian, slouched over with a tray of cups in her hand. "I'm sorry, Hadley, I just can't handle it by myself. I mean, my naturopath really really advised me to keep away from stressful situations and I'm having my period and not feeling very well anyway and I never thought that working in a cafe would... "

"Okay, okay, Lillian." Hadley unfolded her long limbs and took the load of cups. She looked sorrowfully at me. "I think you'd better go on home without me, Pam. I may be here until closing. See you, Miko."

I didn't think Hadley had seen Miko almost begin to cry and I wasn't sure if I had either. She had pulled herself together slightly.

"Miko, what's upsetting you so much?"

"It was just that, that evening. At my place. Afterwards." Miko was crying in earnest now. Mascara ran down her cheeks like coal deposits, and it was hard to understand what she was saying.

"Nicky and Oak stayed and we drank a bottle of wine and had a long discussion about S/M. And they kept saying, I should try it. I'd really like it. So finally I said okay and we went to Oak's house, she has a whole set-up in her basement. I mean, really like a torture chamber. I got completely freaked out. I mean, I was a little drunk, but not that drunk, so finally they gave up trying to persuade me and we went into the living room and then Oak went to bed and I was going to give Nicky a ride back to her place and then, I don't know, Nicky and I ended up making love. Not S/M stuff, just regular stuff, it was wonderful. I felt so fantastic afterwards, I went home feeling really happy and peaceful... And now she's dead. I can't help thinking that Oak killed her and I'm so frightened. I don't know what to do."

"Why do you think that Oak killed her?" I said, trying to take it in. Was any of this plausible, at all? Was a woman who so fervently espoused S/M likely to make vanilla love with someone in her partner's house? Could Miko be making this all up for her own purposes? "Why?" I repeated.

"Nicky wanted to leave her. She told me when I gave her a ride home. She told me a lot of things."

"Do you have any reason to think that Oak might have killed Loie? Had Loie and Nicky ever been involved?"

"Loie and Nicky!" said Miko, completely astounded.

"Is that totally impossible? They knew each other years ago, after all."

Miko was shaking her head. "I don't understand any of this. I shouldn't be talking to you anyway, I should really be talking to the police. Shouldn't I?"

"Well," I said. "Only if you're sure. After all, accusing Oak could really open up a can of worms. The papers are already having a field day with Nicky's job as an exotic dancer. Can you imagine what would happen if the media got hold of a torture chamber? Your name would be dragged right into it, you know. I'm not saying you shouldn't be talking to the police—but you'd better be pretty careful of what you say and how you say it."

"Christ," said Miko, shaken, obviously seeing the headlines float before her: SCHOOL EMPLOYEE IN S/M LOVE TRIANGLE.

"What should I do? What should I do?" Miko was groaning.

"What do you say we take a little drive?" I said.

"Where? Why?"

"To see Oak. She's unlikely to try to kill both of us. And maybe we could find out a few things. Like whether she even knew you and Nicky did it."

Oak lived in the Central District, not far from Providence Hospital. Miko and I drove in separate cars, so I didn't get a chance to ask her some of the questions that kept coming into my mind.

I wasn't surprised that Miko had been persuaded into a closer look at S/M. After all, she was interested in exploring the whole subject of sex, her own fantasies as well as others, so it was probably natural that when the opportunity asserted itself she would take advantage of it. Perhaps she'd even created the opportunity herself, by inviting Nicky and Oak to her video screening.

But would Miko have gone so far as to make love with Nicky in Oak's own living room, while Oak was asleep? And would Oak, if she found out about it, be so angry that she would kill Nicky? The news reports had said that Nicky had been discovered in an alley behind the Fun Palace in the early hours of the morning. If Oak had been the murderer, would she have been likely to do it there, instead of someplace where she could control the situation better? The alley indicated a surprise attack. And if Oak had killed Nicky, according to my theory, she must have also killed Loie. But what possible reason would Oak have for killing Loie? And how would she have had time? My thoughts jumped around. Could Oak have been the person in the classroom who was threatening Loie with consequences if she told? If Loie told the audience that she and Nicky had once been involved? Maybe that was in Loie's manuscript too.

Miko pulled up behind me and we went up to the neatly kept, dark-painted house.

"Who is it?" asked a subdued and cautious voice.

"Miko and Pam Nilsen."

Oak opened the door, not slowly, but with a jerk. "What do you want?"

I started to say, "To ask you some questions," but Miko suddenly broke down and threw herself at Oak. "I can't believe she's dead. I'm so sorry, Oak."

I hadn't imagined tears being part of Oak's hardcore image, but suddenly she was crying too, not easily and dramatically like Miko, but in a kind of stunned, quiet way. For the first time I looked at her without her leathers on and realized that she was much younger than I'd thought, in her mid to late twenties. She was medium height, stocky, with a strong torso. Under her tee-shirt her breasts were small, like those of a fat man. And her face was almost pretty, with a cleft chin and dark blue eyes. I hadn't noticed that at all before. I'd only seen the leather jacket and pants.

Oak finally let us come inside. The small living room was surprisingly old-fashioned, the furniture and decor from the thirties. It looked as if it had been passed on intact from an older generation: lace doilies under ceramic pots; a braided rug, twin armchairs, twin end tables, twin lamps. The only thing that was modern in the room was a large TV set and VCR and behind it, rows and rows of video cassettes.

It was hard to believe there was a torture chamber downstairs. I told myself I didn't want to see it, but of course I did.

Oak sat down in one of the armchairs. Grief had come out like measles all over her face, blotching her fair skin. She said, "Until you got here I was just feeling relieved. Neither the police or the newspapers have connected me with Nicky. I guess I was just in a state of shock. I found out like everyone else—on the news last night. I don't want the cops to come, but it feels like, unless they do, nothing has really happened."

"So Nicky didn't live here then?" I asked.

"No—she had her own apartment, downtown. She didn't stay there much, but she needed it for being alone sometimes, and for sex."

"You mean—she was a prostitute?"

Oak looked at me as if I were crazy. "I said for sex—with her other lovers."

I felt Miko freeze beside me on the sofa.

"We had an agreement," Oak said. "Mondays and Thursdays we both saw other people if we wanted."

"Did that work out for you?" I asked.

Oak nodded. "Yeah. Nicky and I had been together for about three years. The S/M was there from the beginning, but after a year or so the romance started to go. We had the choice to let the whole thing slide or figure out new ways to deal with it. So that's what we decided." Oak wiped the last of her tears from her eyes.

Miko said, "I don't know how to tell you this, Oak, but last Thursday..."

"I know all about it."

"Nicky told you then?"

"She didn't have to," Oak said and for the first time she smiled a little. "I watched it."

"You *watched* it?"

Oak seemed apologetic but she was still smiling. "Nicky had these ideas sometimes. It was her idea to bring you to my house in the first place, to see if we could get you to see what we saw in S/M. Then when you got freaked out and left the basement Nicky said she still thought she could seduce you. I said I doubted it. So she told me to pretend to go to sleep and then come to the top of the stairs in an hour."

"I don't believe you," said Miko. Her round face had gone dark red. "She said she was fed up with you—she wanted to leave you. What happened was a natural thing between us. She would never have suggested it to you. If you did watch us—and I doubt it—I'm sure it was your own sick idea."

"Then why did Nicky get you in that weird position just inside the living room, on the floor then? Why didn't you make love on the couch?"

Miko looked up at the door to the living room with its clear view to the landing. She seemed completely humiliated.

I intervened. "The important question is—Who killed Nicky—and why?" I didn't think we could assume it was Oak in a jealous rage, unless she was totally dissimulating now.

"It must have been a customer at the Fun Palace," Oak said. "In the beginning when she started working there I used to pick her up at night. But after a while she told me not to bother. Shit, those guys are animals, some of them."

"But don't you think it had any relationship to Loie's death?" I said. "They were both killed by dog collars. Where is Nicky's dog collar?"

"Umm," said Oak, stalling.

I'd deliberately said nothing about the leash, about Nicky and Loie most probably having been surprised by the leash and strangled before the dog collar was fastened on.

"Did Nicky give her dog collar to someone?"

Oak looked worried. "Not exactly."

"What happened to it then?"

"She had it in the pocket of her leather jacket. Someone took it out."

I couldn't help sounding a little skeptical. "When was that?"

"When we were at dinner. Nicky hung it up in the restaurant. On the way back to Seattle University she discovered it was gone."

I remember seeing Nicky hang up her coat in the Ethiopian resaturant, but I still felt skeptical. "Why didn't Nicky tell me any of this?" I asked, and Miko added, "It's a little hard to believe."

"Well, it's true," Oak said and was stubbornly silent.

I changed the subject. "I understand that Nicky and Loie knew each other in college."

"They did more than know each other," Oak said.

"What do you mean? Were they lovers?"

"Loie and Nicky? No, Loie was strictly het then. But she needed extra money I guess and she got involved in making porn movies. Then she recruited Nicky and some other people. That's how Nicky got into the business. She used to laugh sometimes about what a hypocrite Loie was. She said it would really be a big surprise for the world if people found out."

Loie—acting in porn movies? The mind reeled. "But don't you see?" I said excitedly. "That's a perfect motive for killing Nicky. Because she knew that about Loie."

"Aren't you forgetting," said Miko, apparently over the first shock of finding out she'd been seduced for a purpose, "That Loie was murdered first? If Loie was already dead then what did it matter what Nicky knew?"

"Who were the other people that Loie recruited?" I asked Oak. "Do you know?"

"I don't know. College types, I guess. Nicky used to joke about it sometimes. The idea of Loie becoming such a puritan after what she'd done."

My mind flashed back to Loie's speech at the end of the workshops. Was that what Loie had been about to reveal? That she'd acted in porn films? "Did Nicky keep a copy of those movies?"

"I don't think so. She had some other videos she'd done for fun since then. I could show you those."

"No thanks," I said, looking at the rows of videos on the shelf behind the TV.

"I wonder if Loie had a copy... " I thought aloud. And to myself I wondered if that was the reason Loie's things had been burgled from Hanna's house. Because Hanna noticed the missing manuscript and notes we had all assumed that that was what the thief was after. But even an unfinished manuscript was nothing to what porn films featuring Loie Marsh would be.

I snapped back. Miko and Oak were staring warily at each other, caught up in feelings of mingled antagonism and grief. They had a lot to sort out.

They hardly noticed when I left.

15

I ARRIVED AT PORTAGE BAY after dark. The long wooden walk down to the houseboat swayed in the black water. I stood a moment by the side of the house and watched the way the small waves captured the reflected light. The old rowboat banged softly against the deck, reminding me that it had been a while since I'd taken it out. Maybe this weekend.

Hadley was in the kitchen making dinner. Red snapper baked in a sauce of tomatos, cilantro and white wine.

"Penny called," she said. "And Elizabeth Ketteridge returning your call. And Gracie London."

"What'd she want?"

"Didn't say. Penny and Ray want you to baby-sit Wednesday." I tried Gracie's number, but only got her answering machine. Then I called Penny and agreed to watch Antonia Wednesday evening and maybe all day Sunday as well.

Finally I called Elizabeth. She sounded pleased to hear from me, but as professional as ever. "Did you decide if you wanted to make an appointment, Pam?"

"Er, no, not exactly. It's just that—I've got a couple of questions."

"Yesss?" she said.

"You probably can't tell me this, but was Loie ever a client of yours?"

"No," she said, sounding relieved. "Loie wasn't."

"Okay. The second thing I'm interested in is if you know a therapist named Clea Florence."

Elizabeth hesitated. "I don't know if Clea would be the right person for you to see, Pam. She's a little—spiritual. And she's got a reputation."

"For what? For having been into S/M?"

"No. I don't think many people knew about that until the conference. No, it's just a reputation... All right, I'll tell you," Elizabeth said. "Clea has apparently slept with a few clients, she's had some scenes in public places, she just isn't able to keep boundaries very well. She really shouldn't be practicing—she doesn't have a degree in psychology or social work. She gets away with it some-how, maybe by charging low fees, or maybe by calling her-self a healer. I know a number of women who've gone to her and not been very happy. There, now I've said my piece. I'll give you her phone number if you still want it."

"Yes please."

She sighed and gave me the number. "If it doesn't work out, Pam, please call me."

"Thanks, Elizabeth. Bye."

Hadley and I sat down to dinner.

"How's the investigation going?" she asked.

"It'd be easier if things didn't keep happening. Hanna called today and said Loie's manuscript had been stolen, her manuscript and half her notes. I've been trying to think all day who could have taken it and why."

"Pauline of course."

"But that's so obvious. She's the first person anyone would suspect. I'm sure Hanna has told the police about Pauline and Loie."

"Maybe Hanna took the manuscript herself and is

trying to pin it on Pauline."

"Too obvious again, though an interesting theory. I've also thought that one of the anti-porn women might have stolen it, just to make sure it got published. Or even," I blushed a little, "Gracie London. She's writing a book on the same subject, maybe she wanted to scope out the competition."

"I thought she could do no wrong?"

"Well, it's not as if I think Gracie would actually kill Loie or Nicky. . . . "

Hadley let my hesitation hang there a moment before she laughed. "No, Gracie seems more subtle than that. So what else have you found out?"

"Miko and I went to see Oak," I told her. "Did you know Miko and Nicky had gotten involved—or anyway, they got it on once —after the video screenings last week?"

"Humph," Hadley said non-committally.

"Miko thought Oak might have killed Nicky out of jealousy. Miko said Nicky had told her she wanted to leave Oak. But Oak made it sound as if the whole thing had been staged for her benefit. I wonder if that was just something Nicky said, about wanting to leave Oak, or if she meant it?"

"I don't know. But it sounds as if Oak and Nicky were non-monogamous."

"Miko was furious," I said.

"She's more romantic than she comes across," Hadley said. Her voice sounded strained. She forked a carrot but didn't eat it.

"Hadley. What aren't you telling me?"

She put down her fork and flipped her hair behind her ears. "Well, I suppose I had to tell you sometime."

"Oh no, Hadley!"

"Calm down. Nothing happened. It's just that—at the conference, Miko got me aside and asked if I'd consider sleeping with her. I admit it, I was attracted to her. Not lots, but enough to make the idea seem interesting. I didn't say no. I said I'd think about it."

I waited.

"I did think about it. I thought about it for a week or so. Remember our conversation at the Copacabana?"

I nodded.

"Well, I was about to tell you then. But after we talked I realized how much it would hurt you. You wouldn't think of it as a little fling, which is all I wanted. If I did sleep with Miko either I'd have to tell you or Miko would go around blabbing it so you'd find out. Either way," Hadley sighed, "it would have probably been the end of our relationship."

She picked up her fork again. "And then we went over to Moe and Allen's and talked about tricking and I just realized it would never work out."

"How do you know that?"

Hadley looked at me in surprise. "I thought you'd be happy when I told you I'd decided monogamy was best."

"I want you to be in a relationship with me because you love me, not because you're afraid of hurting me."

"I do love you," she said. "I thought that was the point."

I got up from the table, no longer hungry. "Well, what if *I* want to be non-monogamous?"

"With whom?" she demanded.

"Nobody. Just in theory. I mean, after the romance dies down. . . "

"Oh, so now the romance has died down, has it?" Her long legs pursued me into the living room, where I'd flopped into a chair. She wasn't angry, just bewildered.

I felt a little bewildered too. It was as if the houseboat had suddenly become unmoored and we were drifting around in unknown seas.

"Well, you have to admit we don't have sex as often as we used to," I said. "And we always do the same things."

"It has gotten a little boring," Hadley admitted. "Much as I like your body. And sometimes I worry you're going to flip me over the side of the bed if I make too sudden a movement."

145

"Oh, that was one time, that was months ago. No, the problem is, we've grown set in our ways. And we know each other too well. We can't act out strange fantasies with each other."

"What strange fantasies?" she asked interestedly.

I began to turn red. "Oh, I don't know."

"No, really. What's the most taboo thing you can think of?"

"Well," I said. "Sometimes I still think about men—you know—sexually. . . . "

I waited for her to be revolted.

"That's not so strange," she scoffed. "So do I sometimes."

"But you were never heterosexual!"

"So? I slept with a few guys in college. Besides, the point of fantasies is that you don't have to act on them. You can just have them."

"Then what's taboo for you?" I moved over to the sofa where she was and put her huge bony feet, endearingly shod in socks with little red Christmas trees, on my lap.

"I'd like to be a prisoner in a harem," she said dreamily.

"What? With a sheik?"

"No dummy. With forty women all in various states of undress. All different colors and sizes and shapes of women, doing nothing all day except perfuming themselves, listening to Bessie Smith records, bathing in bubble bath and eating Belgian chocolate ice cream bars. I'd be a prisoner there and at first I'd try desperately to get out. I'd almost succeed, then they'd capture me again. They'd take my clothes away. And gradually I'd get to like it there. . . . "

"That's a good one," I said admiringly. "I've always wanted to do it in a plane or a train or something. With a lot of people around, but all of them asleep. Though we wouldn't know that for sure. Someone could just pretend to be sleeping."

"I did it once in a plane," Hadley said, putting her

enormous Christmas-treed toe into the crotch of my jeans and starting to move it up and down. "I was on a night flight from New York to Houston during spring break in college. I was seated next to this classy older woman. At least she seemed a lot older—she was probably only thirty-five, if that. I was twenty-one. We started talking—she was a buyer at Neiman Marcus and she asked me a lot about Vassar, especially about the crowd I moved in—and we had some wine with our dinners, and the lights went down, and the blankets came out. . . . We were still talking, and all of a sudden she was playing with the palm of my hand. Really slow, with her thumb. It went on for ever. She didn't want to kiss, maybe that would have been too obvious if a stewardess came by. Instead, after about an hour of this thumb massage, and wriggling around and starting to touch each other through our clothes, she suddenly pulled up her dress, pulled down her pantyhose and put my fingers right down *here*." Hadley increased the pressure of her toe. "I'll never forget it, the woman wasn't wearing anything under her pantyhose."

"Really?" I said. "Good god, and she was a buyer at Neiman Marcus."

"Strange but true."

We devoted ourselves to pleasure for a while and then I said, raising my head for a breather, "Why is the idea of anonymous sex a turn-on?"

"I beg your pardon? This is Hadley, remember me?"

"I was speaking more theoretically. I was thinking about what it would be like to go into the backroom of a bar and. . . . "

"I think some lesbian bars now have backrooms, at least in Berlin."

"I don't think I could do it. Even in Germany. Am I really such a prude?"

"Maybe you just like to keep your fantasies in your head, where they're free and accessible. You haven't even told me what they are, by the way."

"I've had this one," I said dreamily. "Maybe it comes

from living in the Northwest and being cold and wet a lot. Anyway, in this fantasy I'm lying on a beach. I'm alone, maybe listening to some music, baking under the hot sun. I'm sweating and applying suntan oil. I can't quite reach the middle of my back though, and suddenly I hear this very sultry voice saying, 'Let me help you reach the hard spots,' and then her hands are all over me."

"Your bathing suit has mysteriously vanished by this time," Hadley suggested.

"I don't think I was ever wearing one."

"Well, I just hope you remember the hole in the ozone layer and don't stay out there too long." Hadley laughed and pulled me back down.

"This evening reminds me of one of the workshops I went to at the conference," Hadley said later.

"It was a hands-on workshop?"

"No you fool—I mean the talking not the other. It was that boring lecture on Edward Donnerstein's research. But during the discussion period a woman got up and said some really interesting things about erotic romance novels. I haven't ever read any, but apparently there are millions and millions of them being read by women and apparently they're no longer the Barbara Cartland "I was a fragile blond secretary and he raped and brutalized me but I love him" variety, but many of them present sex in a very passionate woman-centered way. Telling the guy what to do, getting on top of him, making sure she gets hers. Anyway, one of the interesting things this woman said was that these books prove the theory that women get turned on with their brains, whereas men tend to get turned on with their bodies. She quoted some anthropological study that suggests that primitive females had to maintain their sex drive beyond estrus in order to keep men around to help with the kids, so they evolved brains that could release hormones to keep them horny. So, unlike men, who have a purely reflective response, women's road to sexual arousal proceeds through the brain. Hence the popularity of fantasy for women.... Pam, honey, are you still awake?"

"Hadley," I said. "Are you telling me that you made up that story about the buyer from Neiman Marcus?"

"Actually," said Hadley, "she was a countess with tawny tresses and a lavish bosom barely restrained in a torn buccaneer's shirt and she was in flight from her dreadful husband the count and she was so grateful to me for saving her that... "

The phone rang, and I reluctantly got up to answer it. I thought it might be Gracie returning my call, but it was Penny again.

"Did you see the Eleven O'Clock News?"

"No, why? What happened?"

"They arrested Pauline for Loie's murder. Oh Pam, it was terrible. The reporter didn't know how to put it, so he said she was Loie's former roommate in Boston and her literary rival. Apparently she'd stolen the manuscript of the book Loie was working on."

"You're right," I told Hadley. "I guess Pauline wasn't worried about being obvious."

16

"Poor Pauline," I couldn't help exclaiming several times the next morning. Each time I did, someone reprimanded me, "Poor Pauline! She killed Loie Marsh, remember?"

I had to agree. There didn't seem to be much doubt. According to Penny, who got it all from Hanna, not only had the police found Loie's manuscript and notes in Pauline's motel room, but they had conclusive proof in the form of an airline ticket that Pauline had arrived in Seattle the afternoon of the conference. The flight bag at the memorial service had been nothing but a cover-up.

There was no doubt at all... and yet there were several things that bothered me. One was that, strictly speaking, it wasn't just Loie's manuscript and notes. If one were to believe Pauline, then the notes and probably the manuscript were more Pauline's than Loie's, so it was no wonder she felt she had a right to them, and that she had tried to get them back. It didn't have to mean that Pauline had killed Loie to get them back. Secondly, even if Pauline had killed Loie, why would she have killed Nicky? Pauline had only been arrested for one murder, yet, according to Sandy's reporter sources, the detectives thought the same person had killed both women.

There was always the possibility that Nicky had seen Pauline kill Loie, but if so, why wait so long to kill her?

The evidence of the plane ticket was damning, obviously, but again, there might be another explanation. Why shouldn't Pauline have wanted to be at a conference where she suspected Loie might try to claim all the glory for herself? But clearly after Loie was murdered there was a good reason for Pauline not to say she'd been there incognito.

I found it curious that Hanna had claimed Edith Marsh had called Pauline to tell her about Loie's murder and that Pauline had denied it. But if Mrs. Marsh had actually talked to Pauline, then that meant Pauline had to have been in Boston, not here. Could someone else have set Pauline up for the murder by using her name to buy the airline ticket. Someone who knew how much Pauline had come to hate Loie?

I didn't think it would hurt to drop by Edith Marsh's house for a short visit, but first I wanted to pay a visit to Clea Florence. I didn't want to give up on the S/M angle without some further investigation. Without much difficulty I made an appointment with her for three o'clock and left work early, telling Penny I had a headache.

Clea Florence was thin, with dark olive skin and sharp white teeth. She could have been Italian, but her tan may have also been the result of too many hours at the electric beach. She had honey-colored hair and pale hazel eyes. She was wearing a brightly colored green and pink tunic and a great deal of turquoise and rose crystal jewelry. She had a small calico bag on a string around her neck, and a unusual half-medicinal, half-earthy smell seemed to emanate from it.

"Hello, hello," she greeted me at the door of her living room and made me comfortable on a pillow. The room was dim and filled with pillows and photographs. There were no books on her shelves, only stones and rocks.

"So?" she said, when we were settled. I saw she meant to be kind and welcoming, but the abruptness of the question unnerved me a little. I had a feeling that she worked very hard at giving an impression of strength and calmness, but in her eyes was the tensed look of a cat watching a catnip mouse swing back and forth.

"Well," I said. "Uh. Maybe you could give me a some idea of the kind of therapy you do."

"It depends," she said. "What you want help with. Is it a relationship, family, old memories?"

"Old memories," I said. That seemed innocuous enough. After all, didn't everybody have old memories?

"I see," Clea nodded. "Well, it depends on you really. I'm not a traditional therapist, you know, though we will do lot of talking too. I use healing stones, a little aromatherapy, some dreamwork. I don't think of myself as a therapist, more as a psychic guide. So there are a number of things we can do. We can make art, write, dance... "

I coughed slightly.

"Does something amuse you?" she asked.

"Oh—I guess I've just never heard of dancing therapy."

"It can be a very healing experience to get in touch with your creative, spiritual self," she reprimanded me.

"Look, Clea, I should say I'm here because I heard you at the sexuality conference talking about having been into S/M and I wanted to know more about it."

From the look in her eyes I thought she was going to blast me out of the water, but suddenly she grew kind again. "You want to get out too, is that it?"

"Well... "

"I guess I've been learning a lot this week about coming out as a former sadomasochist," she said. "Maybe that's going to be part of my work as a therapist. Up until recently I haven't been able to talk about it. But I found it really painful to hear Nicky and Oak saying things I *know* aren't true."

Clea tucked her knees under her and touched the calico bag hanging around her neck. "I grew up expecting sex to be rough and liking to be dominated. Those were the first fantasies I had. I'd had fantasies like that with men, but I struggled—successfully—against acting on them. I finally got into S/M with a woman lover back in the late seventies, early eighties when everybody was talking about it and saying how great it was. Some of my friends came out as masochists or sadists, and my lover admitted that she'd always wanted to take our sexuality a little further. She already was pretty dominant in bed, always on top and taking the lead, but we'd never talked openly about it, never used any toys.

"We started out with scarves and dildos, but before six months was up we were hardcore. We spent hundreds of dollars on props for our scenes and pretty soon all our free time was taken up with this new form of entertainment. The physical pain seemed pretty minimal, I remember laughing sometimes thinking how people focused on that all the time, as if that were really the point of S/M. But S/M was a total consciousness, it wasn't just confined to the physical, it got into all aspects of my relationship with my lover. At first verbal humiliation was a turn-on, later on it got to be constant and more and more degrading.

"I know that some proponents of S/M talk about trading roles back and forth, but we never did, and none of our friends did. We were stuck in our roles, addicted to our roles. There was so much intensity in it that it was hard to go back to so-called vanilla sex. But the violence kept escalating. What I finally had to realize was that I was in an abusive relationship—my lover was a batterer and S/M enabled her to batter and feel good about it.

"When I look back on the experience I see that I was trying to work out a whole series of things that happened to me in my childhood, when I was neglected, humiliated and beaten. The S/M ritual seemed like a way of working out some of that repressed pain, transforming it into something that I chose freely and could control. Other women

153

have talked about S/M as a healing experience or a way of dealing with the emotional S/M in our lives. I can't believe that I ever agreed."

Clea stopped and fingered her rose quartz necklace. "I understand now that you can never heal through violence; you have to love yourself and accept yourself. Re-enacting scenarios compulsively isn't cathartic, it's harmful. Very, very harmful."

"That's what I'm starting to think," I said. "Now that Loie Marsh and Nicky Kay have both been choked by dog collars."

"But Loie Marsh wasn't into S/M!" Clea was shocked.

"How do you know?"

"Aside from the fact that everything she said spoke against the sadomasochistic mentality, I would have known about it. The S/M network is very connected. She could never have kept that quiet."

"That makes me feel better," I said.

"I've told you my story," said Clea encouragingly. "Are you ready to talk about yours?"

I got up. "No, uh, not yet," I said. "But thanks so much for telling me what you told me. It really helped. Really."

"I'll get used to talking about it," said Clea, walking me to the door, "I know I'll get used to it."

I paid her, left and thought it interesting that she didn't dispute that Nicky had been found with a dog collar around her neck, even though the papers had never mentioned it.

My excuse to Edith Marsh was on the weak side: "I'm sorry that my sister and I just ran out like that after the service. So today I was in the neighborhood and I thought I'd just stop in. I hope it's all right. I guess, my parents being Norwegian and all. . . . " I held out a lemon pound cake I'd picked up at Larsen's Bakery.

Edith looked surprised and then so pleased that I almost left right then with a guilty conscience. But she quickly invited me inside and said we must have some cake and coffee.

"Nilsen," she said. "Was that Arne Nilsen's hardware in Ballard?"

"That was my grandfather," I admitted. "My father and mother had a print shop downtown. Sig and Louise Nilsen."

"I knew a Sig once," she said. "But he was killed... Oh," Edith said. "Of course. You poor dear."

She brought me into the living room, filled with the usual pine furniture and woven runner mats. It was cozier than Hanna's house and more expensive.

"Mother," said Edith. "Here's that nice Pam Nilsen from Loie's funeral. She's brought us some lemon pound cake and her father was Sig Nilsen, Arne Nilsen's boy, remember Arne's hardware store, on Market Street?"

Mrs. Sandbakker said of course she did and she launched into an amazing litany of unfamiliar and half-remembered names, while Edith went off to make coffee.

When she returned I mentioned that I'd come straight from work and hoped I wasn't interrupting their dinner hour.

"Oh no," said Edith. "We always eat early, so this is dessert for us. I only work until three, usually. I'm the administrator for a small nursing home. Of course today I didn't go in at all... it was quite a shock."

"It must have been a terrible shock," I agreed.

"Oh, it was. It was." Though she didn't look particularly shocked as she poured out coffee. Perhaps that came from being in nursing or in administration. "The worst has been the reporters. They're paying more interest now than when Loie was killed. At first I wasn't going to open the door to you. I thought you might be that awful woman from *USA Today* who's been lurking around."

"You don't think there's been any mistake then? That Pauline could have done it?"

"My dear, how could the police make a mistake? It's

very clear that that woman murdered my daughter and then tried to steal her book."

I felt a little disturbed by Mrs. Marsh's detached tone. Last week driving away from the memorial service she had been certain that Loie was a victim of random violence. Was it so easy to give that theory up and accept that your daughter had been murdered by her ex-lover?

"One thing I don't quite understand," I said. "You said you called Pauline at home Saturday night after the murder. In Boston."

Edith's large face flushed. "That was a misunderstanding," she said. "I tried to call her, but couldn't get through. Hanna was the one who left a message on Pauline's machine. Of course Pauline didn't get it. She was already here."

"You don't think it could have been anyone else, do you? Her ex-husband? Someone she knew from the past?"

I felt that Mrs. Sandbakker had gone quite still and was observing me closely, but Edith Marsh exclaimed,

"David? What a ridiculous idea. Loie ran his life while they were married and now Sonya runs it. He's not a strong man, David, not like Loie's father."

"Did they meet in college?"

"Yes, they did. David was three years younger than Loie. That was a mistake, from the start. Why would a twenty-three year old girl marry a man so much younger? I always thought that was the root of the problem. For instance if he'd married Hanna. They were the same age and at the time they had the same interests—acting and politics. But he married Loie—she was a beautiful girl then, not quite so big as she later became."

"Loie took him away from Hanna," Mrs. Sandbakker said. I had the uneasy feeling that she saw straight through me, but that for some reason she was encouraging me. It couldn't be because of Grandpa Arne, so why was it?

"Mother! That's ridiculous. No, David is obviously drawn to strong women. Hanna is strong, but she's also weak. And of course now they wouldn't agree about politics at all. Yes, David was drawn to Loie for her strength. As for Loie, I don't know what the attraction was, since we now know she wasn't interested in men at all."

"She wanted to punish Hanna," Mrs. Sandbakker said stubbornly.

Edith Marsh's carmine lips set in a thin line. "You and Erik have always taken Hanna's side in everything."

"Someone had to. Loie was always such a pushy child."

The two women glared at each other. I said, as innocently as possible, "I keep wondering if the death of that woman Nicky Kay had anything to do with Loie's murder. Someone told me that Nicky and Hanna were roommates in college."

"Now there's another story!" Mrs. Marsh burst out. "When I was growing up, you went to school, got married and had children. If you were smart you got some training to fall back on if anything happened, like I did as a nurse. Girls these days are so different. Now Nicky was a perfectly lovely girl, she grew up in Wenatchee and she had never been to Seattle before she came to the University of Washington. Hanna often brought her by to have dinner that first year when they were freshmen. And then you come to find out that all these years she's been working as a... as a prostitute."

Edith hadn't answered my question. I didn't know if that was intentional. I did know that I'd just had two cups of coffee and should be making leaving movements.

I began to gather myself together and said as casually as possible, "Well, I hope the publicity around Loie and Pauline isn't too awful for you. If Pauline talks to reporters I'd be worried what she would say. She seems a little out of control to me."

"I should say!" said Mrs. Marsh. "Did you see the way she behaved at the memorial service? She wasn't even polite."

"You could hardly expect politeness from a murderess," said Mrs. Sandbakker. I looked at her quickly; her tone had been almost ironic.

I got up. "Thank you so much for coffee, Mrs. Marsh. I really should be going. . . I hope Hanna is feeling better, now that they know who did it. She seemed so upset after the memorial service, when you reminded her about Loie saving her life."

I didn't know why but Edith Marsh suddenly looked angry and impatient. "Well, that's just Hanna," she said brusquely. "Always over-emotional about things."

They came with me to the door and we ended our visit back at Arne Nilsen and the days when belonging to the Sons of Norway had really *meant* something.

I hoped our shared Scandinavian heritage would keep me in their good graces and that they wouldn't think too hard about the meaning of my visit.

Though I suspect that Mrs. Sandbakker, at least, already had.

It was only six-thirty and I knew that Hadley wouldn't be home yet, so I decided to stop off at the university and see if I could find out anything more about the college careers of Loie, Hanna, Nicky and David. I decided I'd look through back issues of the *Daily*, the University of Washington newspaper, from the one year when they'd all been at the university together.

In Suzzallo library I microfiched forward and back, feeling at times a little sting of jealousy. I was sorry not to have been part of the student movement in its prime. Students were still demonstrating by the time Penny and I arrived at the university, but it was all getting a little passe.

All of a sudden I stopped. There was a photo of Hanna Sandbakker, looking incredibly young, her hair falling straight and blond from a center part, her lips pale and her eyes dark in the fashion of the day. She had just appeared in a production at the Glen Hughes Playhouse of *Mrs. Warren's Profession* as Evie Warren. It was her debut performance, the glowing review said, and she had completely eclipsed all the other players. I looked at the end of the review to see what other actors were mentioned. "Loie Marsh was adequate as Mrs. Warren, but her tendency to overact was even more apparent next to Hanna Sandbakker's freshness and originality."

So Loie had acted too. No one had mentioned that before. I spun the dial forward looking for reviews of other plays that winter and spring. There was Hanna Sandbakker's name, over and over, the fledging drama critics predicting a glorious acting career for her. There was no further mention of Loie Marsh. Had her acting been a transitory thing then? She'd ended up teaching drama in a Kirkland high school, but that was what you did if you had a drama degree and couldn't make it in the theater. I searched the reviews for other names I recognized, and there, in a review of *Hedda Gabler* I found David Gustafson as Tesman. "Captures the part of the well-meaning husband perfectly." Also making her first appearance on the stage was Sonya Rees as Thea Elvsted. I wondered if it was the same Sonya that David had eventually married. It must be. She'd said she'd known them all slightly back then.

My eyes were beginning to ache, but I thought it couldn't hurt to turn back another year and see if Loie had appeared in any other plays. I found her name mentioned in two productions. The reviews were kind, rather than spectacular. Still, they weren't completely discouraging, not for someone who really wanted to believe she could act. They weren't like the damning comparison with Hanna in *Mrs. Warren's Profession*.

I was starting to put some things together. There were ties among these people that went back years, and yet none of them now seemed to like each other or to have remained in contact. Nicky had been Hanna's roommate, but had gone off in a completely different direction. Hanna had humiliated Loie and her dreams of acting, and Loie, to get back at her, had married David, the man Hanna loved—

according to Mrs. Sandbakker at least. Sonya seemed to have played a fairly peripheral part—still, you never knew.

Added to this was the scurrilous suggestion that Loie and Nicky had been in a porn film together. But what was the name of the film and what had happened to it? And even if I managed to locate it what were the chances it would tell me anything I needed to know? It wouldn't have mattered particularly to Nicky if Loie had talked publicly about the film. Loie was the one it would hurt.

I left the library and went out to my car. Red Square was filled with students on their way to evening classes, walking in groups, carrying books. I felt transported for an instant back into my own student past. It was funny how strong emotions were then, how much we assumed we knew everything. Our relationships were intense and they seemed as if they'd last forever. I still had that feeling about some of the people I knew from that time.

I wondered if the murderer did too.

17

By the next day the papers had managed to dig up a good angle on Pauline's arrest. Suddenly *We Took Back the Night* was a modern feminist classic and Loie Marsh the martyred heroine of the anti-porn movement. Pauline was so far not talking to the press from jail, but the newspapers still had managed to find out a lot about her. It was essentially the same information Pauline had given me, but it sounded worse by the time it appeared in an exclusive story in *The Seattle Times*. Pauline was suddenly "an untalented hanger-on," Loie's "live-in lover" who was "furious at being abandoned."

Mrs. Marsh was quoted several times, as were some prominent feminists and activists in the anti-porn movement who said that Loie's murder was just an example of the lengths people would go to shut up the voice of truth. Ignoring the fact that it was actually a sister anti-porn activist who was accused of murdering Loie, one prominent New York feminist spoke bitterly of "the backlash of sexual liberalism" and the gains of the women's movement being "viciously eroded."

I supposed it was pedantic to ask how an erosion could be vicious.

Hanna, meanwhile, had removed herself from the fray and was refusing to speak to anyone from the media. She was staying with her father and rehearsing for a new production of a Sam Shepard play.

We talked about her on Wednesday night when I arrived at Penny's and Ray's to fulfill my baby-sitting promise.

"When did Hanna get involved in politics?" I asked Penny as she dressed in the bedroom.

"Oh, she's been active for years. In one thing and another. But I think going to Nicaragua was a real catalyst for her, as well as for us. It's one thing to read about an economic boycott—it's another to see everything rigged together with wire and string and bits of this and that because they can't get parts to fix anything. Hanna has been fundraising non-stop ever since our group came back. Mainly for spare parts for ambulances."

"Do you think she's working herself too hard?" I suggested. "You said you thought she was highly strung."

"Certain things can set her off," Penny admitted. "But she's not some kind of temperamental artist."

"Did she ever talk about Loie to you?"

"You mean in Nicaragua? No. Other people would sometimes talk about their relatives; it made you realize how fragile life was when every day you met people who'd lost family. But Hanna never did."

Penny looked at me. We were both remembering our parents, and how we found it so difficult to talk about them. There never seemed to be the right moment. We never made the right moment.

We didn't make it now either, but went into my former bedroom, which had become Antonia's. It was hardly recognizable for all the duckling-printed curtains and pictures of animals on the walls. The room was packed with the paraphernalia of babydom: diapers, blankets, bottles. From the seriousness with which Penny began to explain how it all worked you would have thought they were planning to go away for six months rather than three or four hours. But in the midst of it all Penny suddenly stopped and said, "Remember I told you I couldn't remember what set off Hanna's outburst that first night in Managua?"

"Yes."

"It's come back to me. One of the men in the group was a real admirer of Hanna's. He said he'd seen all her plays. She was very sweet about it; she said a couple of times that he probably hadn't seen everything, because she'd done a considerable amount of work in Minneapolis at the Guthrie Theater over the years. He was kind of a pathetic jerk really. I suppose he thought he was flattering her, because he went on and on and finally he said he'd seen her movies too. At first Hanna very politely said she hadn't made any movies and then when he insisted, she flew into the kind of hysterical fit we saw after the funeral. I think she was just overtired and the prospect of having some idiot around for six weeks who was going to make her life miserable was too much. We all talked to the guy and the next day Hanna was fine. She even apologized to the poor schmuck."

"Hmmmm," I said, rather distracted by the sight of Antonia beginning to fidget. "I thought you told me she was going to sleep the whole time?"

"Yes, yes, she *is* asleep," said Penny, moving hastily to the door where Ray was waiting. "I've left you our number, but she should be fine. See you in a few hours. And thanks, Pam!"

I approached Antonia gingerly. Our neighbor Mrs. Mortensen had claimed she looked exactly like Penny and me when we were small. I didn't see how you could tell—it had been years and years and besides, she had very black straight hair and Ray's almond-shaped eyes. Maybe there was something familiar about the round little chin; there wasn't enough of it to judge.

She was so tiny, midget hands, miniscule ears. I had a great longing to pick her up and hold her close. It made me feel a little mawkish. I didn't want to have children myself, I'd never really wanted to. Still, the thought of Antonia looking a little bit like me and at the same time being a separate person with her whole life before her, was very touching. It brought back shivery sensations of what it must have felt like when I was a baby. Had my fingernails really been that pink and fresh? My skull that fragile? I thought of the casual way Penny and Ray had taken to throwing her around. Had our parents treated us like that? And not like vulnerable little dolls? My first memory had been of my sister's face, of somehow realizing she was different from me.

I'd brought along a book Gracie had lent me, *The History of Sexuality* by Michel Foucault, but I didn't read it. I sat in that bedroom and watched Antonia sleep for three hours.

Who said being an aunt was hard?

It wasn't until I was on the way home that the significance of what Penny had told me about Hanna sunk in. Oak had said that Loie had been in porn films and had gotten Nicky to appear in them too. But Nicky was Hanna's roommate and it seemed clear that Nicky and Loie met through Hanna. Wasn't it likely then that Hanna had also been in a porn film at some point and that was why she was so upset about the well-meaning guy in Managua? She probably lived with the fear of being exposed someday. Yet if that was so, why would she be afraid of Loie exposing her? Loie had more to lose than Hanna if it came out she'd acted in porn films. Or was it Nicky who had planned to expose both of them?

It was difficult to try to trace events that went back so far, especially when two of the main characters were now dead. That their deaths had something to do with past events I was pretty sure, but I wasn't sure what course to take next. I could look for the evidence—the porn films themselves—yet even finding them might leave unanswered questions. Had Miko been lying when she said Nicky wanted to leave Oak, or was it Oak who wasn't telling the truth. Was Pauline just an innocent who'd been done wrong or had she calculated exactly what she was doing? I thought I might have ruled out a few suspects, but new suspicions surrounded everyone who was left.

When I got back home Hadley said that Gracie London had called again and left no message. It was too late to return her call, and when I tried the next morning I got her answering machine again.

I had decided to try to sneak up on the problem by visiting Pauline in jail, both to decide for myself whether I thought Pauline had killed Loie, if not Nicky, and to discover if Pauline knew anything more about Loie's past. She'd been genuinely surprised and upset that Loie had been married and clearly Loie had never encouraged Pauline to come to Seattle, where she might have discovered another Loie than the one Loie had presented. Still, Loie might have confided something.

Pauline hadn't been able so far to meet her bail and she hadn't yet decided on a lawyer to represent her. She'd been taken into custody at the motel where she was staying and charged with Loie's murder based on her possession of the manuscript and notes for *We Took Back the Night* and on the time of her plane ticket to Seattle. I assumed it was Hanna who had tipped off the police. If the detectives who arrested her had found anything else suspicious among Pauline's possessions, a dog collar and leash, for instance, nobody was saying.

She came into the visitors' area to greet me looking better than I'd ever seen her. Either she was relieved to have been found out or else life in the King County Jail agreed with her. The pinched look around her eyes and mouth was gone and her hunched shoulders were relaxed. The

165

crumpled ball of paper was unfolding; even her voice was less adenoidal.

It was probably the most attention she'd gotten in years.

She said, with some relish, "It's been horrible, of course. Eventually they'll find out I didn't do it, but it's going to take time. I've tried to explain over and over that I only took what was rightfully mine. If they'd only look, they'd see that most of the notes are in my handwriting. That's all I wanted. For justice to be done. The book was as much mine as hers and now she's dead, who else but me could carry on the work?"

"So you're not saying that you didn't break into Hanna's?"

"It wasn't hard," bragged Pauline. "The bathroom window was wide open. I just crawled in and found the boxes Loie had left."

"And all that was in the boxes were notes and clippings?"

"What else could there be?" Pauline was sharp—or protective?

"I don't know—magazines, video cassettes... "

"I recognized everything in the box—I'd collected most of it myself, and the notes were in my handwriting."

"How far had Loie gotten with writing?"

"An introduction, well, notes for an introduction—an outline really. She didn't mention *me* at all."

"I thought there was a manuscript, Hanna and everyone have talked about a manuscript."

"Loie *would* call what she had a manuscript," Pauline said scornfully. "*I'd* call it a four-page outline. She'd probably written it for the agent and that was as far as she got."

"Did she talk about anyone else? Nicky for instance? Oak? Her family?"

"No," said Pauline, "at least not what I read." She suddenly looked frightened. "I never expected them to arrest me for *murder*. You can't possibly think that I would kill Loie, can you?"

"There seems to be a little circumstantial evidence," I suggested, but mildly, as if to show I didn't believe a word of it.

"I *never* told anybody at the service that I'd just arrived in Seattle from the airport. It was a conclusion they jumped to from seeing my flightbag. If I was going to kill Loie why would I fly to Seattle under my own name? And I certainly wouldn't choose to strangle her in the bushes of Seattle University. I'd had millions of opportunities in Boston. Why would I want to do it in Seattle?"

"Because you didn't want her to speak on the panel?"

"I came to Seattle because I wanted to hear what she was going to say in public about the book," said Pauline. "I couldn't risk coming to the workshops, but I could risk the crowded auditorium at night. I decided, you see, that if Loie said anything negative about me I was going to fight her for the book. I wasn't going to be ignored any longer."

"But when I first met you you said that nobody had told you about Loie's murder. You said that Mrs. Marsh hadn't called, that nobody had called except Hanna to tell you about the memorial service."

"I was calling my answering machine to hear the messages. You just assumed I was in Boston. I got a message from Hanna on Tuesday about the memorial service. I never got one Saturday from Mrs. Marsh."

"Are you sure you weren't in Seattle earlier in the afternoon, when Loie gave her closing speech at the conference?"

"No... why?"

"Because there was a point when Loie seemed to look straight at someone in the audience and change what she was going to say."

"It wasn't me. My flight didn't get in until four."

She would have had time to get there if she'd come directly from the airport. I remembered the crush of people who'd come in after Gracie's speech. Pauline could easily have been among them. I persisted, "Loie seemed about to say something about women who had been forced to undergo degradation. Someone had suggested to me that Loie might have acted in a porn film when she was younger."

Pauline neither denied or accepted it. "Loie found it easy to put herself into the place of victims of pornography. Sometimes she seemed to know a lot about what actually went on in pornography. But she'd done a lot of research, talked to a lot of people."

"Didn't you ever ask her about her own experience? Weren't you concerned that she might have suffered as a victim of pornography herself?"

"We spoke on behalf of pornography victims, we weren't victims ourselves," Pauline said, almost defensively. "Though obviously, any woman can be victimized."

"But did she ever talk about names of films she'd been in or about the people who acted in them with her? Did she have copies?"

"I don't know what you're getting at," Pauline said angrily. "Are you suggesting Loie was blackmailing people?"

"I'm not saying that," I protested, as the warden signaled to Pauline that the period was over.

I watched Pauline as she was led away, wondering once again about Loie's family. Maybe I needed to take another trip to North Seattle.

Mrs. Sandbakker was out working in her garden when I came by. She was thin and spry, her white hair neatly pulled back into a short braid. Loose gabardine slacks belted tightly at the waist and a heavy sweater gave her an elegant look in spite of her work; she was energetically raking leaves away from the beds of squash and cabbage.

She didn't look terribly surprised to see me.

"I thought you'd be back, maybe," she said, and handed me the rake.

"I have more questions," I admitted. "And I'm hoping you might have some of the answers."

Mrs. Sandbakker picked up a hoe and began to turn over the dark earth around one of the big spaghetti squashes. "Every family has secrets," she said. "Some people in the family know them; others don't know them; others know them but don't want anyone else to know them."

"Sometimes it's better to tell secrets," I said. "It can clear the air."

"Your own secrets, perhaps. But what about other people's secrets?"

"You've already mentioned several secrets," I said, a little impatiently. "For instance, you said that Loie took David away from Hanna."

"I think so," she said.

"Because Hanna could act and Loie couldn't, was that the reason? But Loie couldn't have really been in love with him, could she? She left him. Why didn't he marry Hanna then, instead of Sonya?"

"He and Hanna had already changed too much. David had gotten 'saved.' And Hanna really *could* act. Hanna didn't want him anymore."

"How do you know?"

Mrs. Sandbakker pursed her lips. "I just do."

"Is that why Loie always felt so guilty towards Hanna? Or was it for other things—like for putting Hanna in a film?"

Mrs. Sandbakker shook her head. "I don't know anything about any film." She stopped hoeing and looked at me. "Which of us has the right to speak for another? How could Loie speak for Hanna, how could Loie tell Hanna's secret?"

"Maybe it wasn't just Hanna's secret." I was thoroughly confused now.

"It was all of our secret," said Mrs. Sandbakker. "But if Hanna doesn't tell you, then I can't."

"But . . ."

"I've said what I could," said Mrs. Sandbakker. "And it's very late." She finished patting the earth back down around the squash and took my rake. "Good-bye, and good-luck."

There was no way around it. I was going to have to talk to Hanna. However painful it might be to her, however hysterical it might make her, I was going to have to ask her about the porn film.

According to Penny she was in rehearsal for *Fool For Love* at A.C.T. I slipped into the dark theater, hoping no one would ask me my business. But the theater was fairly empty. On stage were only Hanna and a man. The director sat in the front row.

Hanna was wearing a denim skirt and a loose white tee-shirt. She stomped barefoot around the stage, which had only a bed and a table and chair. Her ash-blond hair was in disarray and she had a twangy accent. She talked about love and holding on and letting go. She shouted at the man, who backed down. Then they both threw themselves to the floor; the window of the motel was apparently in danger of being shot out.

The director stopped her a couple of times. Each time she broke off, listened, nodded her head and went on. There was an amazing sense of poise about her. She could travel so easily from thoughtfulness to furious abandon.

After half an hour the director called a break. Hanna sank into one of the front seats and began to read the script again. She seemed not to recognize me at first.

"Penny's sister," I reminded her.

"Oh. What do you want? I'm in rehearsal."

"I haven't been able to get you at home and I wanted to ask you a few questions."

"About what?" She still had the twangy voice of her character. She sounded a little like Hadley in fact, when Hadley was "putting on Texas" as she called it.

"I'm interested in helping fundraise for the ambulances in Nicaragua."

Hanna's face softened and I felt a pang of guilt. I *would* help fundraise, I decided suddenly. Nevertheless it was definitely with ulterior motives that I persevered with my questions about how I could best help the cause. Finally, when I was sure she was no longer on guard, I asked sympathetically,

"All this has been really hard for you, hasn't it? All this about Loie and Pauline and Nicky."

"I feel bad about Pauline," she admitted, now in her normal, velvety voice. "But she *was* the one who stole the manuscript... "

"Pauline said there was no manuscript, just an outline and notes."

Hanna didn't contradict me. "All I know is that someone broke in and took whatever Loie was working on and we know it was Pauline."

"Yes, I'm sure she did it," I said firmly. "Though I don't see what connection there could be between Nicky and Loie."

Hanna's lovely eyes slid away. "Maybe there is none."

"You knew Nicky, didn't you?" I tried to sound indifferent.

"Yes. We were roommates our first year in college. We used to get on really well. But our lives went in different directions. I'm sorry she's dead." Hanna had started out slowly, searching for words, but by the end her comments sounded rehearsed. I wished I knew a way to get under her control.

"It's funny," I said, still indifferently, "how Pauline seemed convinced when I talked to her that nothing had ever happened to Loie personally to make her so anti-porn. Pauline said she and Loie spoke on *behalf* of victims, that they weren't victims themselves. But I was talking to a therapist I know—Elizabeth Ketteridge—and she said she felt Loie was probably a tormented person inside, that it's possible she might have been abused in some way or involved in porn as a. . . "

Hanna interrupted me. "All her life Loie believed that she had the right to speak for other people, to use other people's experiences for her own purposes. No, nothing ever happened to Loie. It would have been better if something had."

"What do you mean? What happened?"

Hanna had been getting more and more agitated, but her outburst was one I didn't expect. "It was *her* father," she said. "Why did he have to pick on me? I suppose because I was always the little one, the one who couldn't defend herself. Loie was always so big and outspoken. She would have told somebody immediately. I didn't feel like I had anybody to tell—my parents were divorced and my mother had gone away with some guy and my dad was completely griefstricken. And then instead of being a steady adult in my life, Uncle Jake took advantage of me. Not of his own daughter—but of *me*."

"How do you know he didn't take advantage of Loie as well?"

"Because I finally told her. After Uncle Jake died. I wanted to find out if it had just been me. And it *had!*"

Hanna was shaking with anger and grief. I tried to comfort her but she shook me off. "And she had the nerve, she had the *nerve* to say she was going to write about me in her book. She was going to use me as a fucking *example*."

I stood there helplessly, hands extended in a futile gesture of comfort. The director came over and very matter-of-factly observed that I was upsetting Hanna and that I should probably leave. I did then, even though I didn't feel I'd gotten answers to some of the questions I'd come with. This was all turning out to be much more complicated than I'd imagined. The ties that had connected, and still connected Hanna and Loie, were complex and hidden. Had Loie become an anti-porn activist out of guilt? To make up for not having protected Hanna at an earlier age? But why had she married Hanna's boyfriend then? Why had she gotten Hanna involved in porn films? Or had it been Hanna who got Loie involved?

I said good-bye to Hanna, feeling terrible that I'd opened up this wound for her again. Though at least, I realized as I left the theater, I now knew which client Elizabeth had been trying to protect.

18

I⊤ WAS DARK BY the time I got to Oak's house. She came
to the door with a beer in her hand.

"Oh hi," she said, and seemed almost glad to see me.
"Come on in. I just got home."

She led me into the old-fashioned living room.

"Where *did* you get all this stuff?" I couldn't help asking.

"My grandmother left it to me, along with the house. I
kind of like it—it seems familiar somehow."

I had a quick pang for the Ravenna house. If I did sell
my share to Penny—and I still wasn't sure I was ready
to—at least I had to have some of the furniture.

Oak sat down across from me in an armchair with
doilies on the arms. She was wearing jeans again and a soft
blue shirt the color of her eyes. I found it hard to believe
that she could enjoy whipping anyone; I thought of Clea's
story and wondered if she'd just been unlucky with her
lover, if they'd gone too far, or if that was always how it
was. Had Oak been battering Nicky? I just didn't think so,
but maybe that was my own naivete.

"I can't help thinking about her all the time," Oak
said. "It's like, any minute she could come walking

174

through the kitchen door telling me some story. Or I could come in and here she'd be reading on the couch."

"Have you heard anything from the police?"

"No. I guess eventually they'll get to me. I went by her place, but it had a seal on the door. I didn't stop."

"Oak," I said. "Remember you told me that Nicky had been in a porn film with Loie?"

"Yeah."

"I'd like to find those films. I think they could help tell us who killed both Loie and Nicky."

Oak looked up at the shelf of cassettes. "Well, Nicky kept all her video stuff here, because I have a VCR and she didn't, but I never saw anything that old. I mean, did they even have video then?"

That was a good question. I didn't know. "Maybe we could just look through the cassettes?"

"Okay."

They were jumbled together. Hollywood action pictures along with pornographic films. Lots were in cases with no labels or in cardboard boxes. "We bought a lot of bootleg tapes," said Oak. "And people copy them, trade them."

She had hundreds. Like most people have books. But I went through all of them, opening up all the cases and the boxes.

Finally I came to an oblong book-shaped box fitted in among the others. When I opened it, it didn't have the usual cassettes inside, but small reels of tape in a plastic bag.

"Can you put these on your video machine, Oak?" I asked.

She took them out of the bag and looked at them. "I don't see how. They're not in a cassette. They're reels. That's funny, I haven't seen them before. What's the box say? Nothing."

"Would you mind very much if I borrowed these?" I asked her.

"What are you going to do with them?"

"Take them to someone who I hope can play them," I said.

Miko held up one of the reels I'd given her. "Where'd you get these?"

"At Oak's. They were in a little box. We couldn't play them on Oak's VCR, so I thought you might be able to do something with them. They might be the porn films we're looking for."

"If they are, they're strictly the work of amateurs," said Miko. "They look like they might be early videos. Maybe Portapak videos."

"What's that?"

"In the late sixties Sony introduced the first video recorder and camera for consumers. It was reel to reel, not cassette. You could get about twenty minutes on a single reel. Black and white, half inch. We had a Portapak in my high school drama department, that's why this looks familiar. It was always breaking down because no one could figure out how to thread the tape through the spools." She held up one of the reels. "I'll take this in to work tomorrow and see what I can make of it."

We were in her studio; I'd come straight here after leaving Oak's. I hadn't gotten a good look at it at her screening; now I began to walk around, noticing the Japanese feeling about the place—advertising Japan rather than simple, elegant Japan. There were pages torn from magazines on the walls, movie stills, big posters. A lot of it represented sex.

"The Japanese have a long tradition of pornography," said Miko, watching me investigate her studio. "I was shocked—yes, even me—when I was in Tokyo a few years ago and saw how sex was used to sell everything. Women's bodies, that is. It gave me very mixed feelings. On the other hand, Japanese rape statistics are supposed to be among the lowest in the world... Would you like some tea?"

176

"Yes, please." I continued to walk around. There were tiny paintings made of silk, fascinating old photographs of women, shelves full of art books, Vermeer as well as Hokusai.

"Surprised?" she asked, when I stopped at the bookshelves. "You think of me as a pretty crass person, don't you, Pammie?"

"You can say some fairly alarming things," I admitted.

"Don't be fooled," said Miko, putting a round ceramic pot and two cups on a low table and gesturing me over. "I'm really quite a wimp. I suppose that's one reason I was drawn to Nicky. She called herself a sexual outlaw and that's what she was. She pushed boundaries, she crossed limits. She was in pursuit of something. I don't feel as courageous. I suppose I'm still rebelling against my parents."

"Maybe Nicky was too," I suggested, but Miko went on:

"My mother was a Japanese war bride, my dad was in the service, your basic redneck sergeant. He used to knock both of us around. I grew up hating him and being ashamed of my mother. Ashamed of anything Japanese. I hated my face, hated my body. I was overweight, I had acne. Kids used to call me Fat Jap and Slanty-Eyes. That was suburban Tacoma in the fifties and sixties. I went to Pacific Lutheran University—did I forget to mention we were good Christians?—for a couple of years, then I couldn't take it anymore. I was a real slut in college. I drank and smoked and slept around."

Miko sipped her tea, looking back into the sorrow and excitement of those years. "I've always wanted to start a support group for women like me. Women Who've Fucked Around, I'd call it. Or maybe Sluts Anonymous. It wouldn't be a survivors' group or anything like that—it would be to really talk about, really understand what it was like. How it was sometimes fabulous, sometimes wretched and a lot of times it meant nothing at all."

"The fucking around was with men, right?" I asked

cautiously.

Miko snorted. "Of course! Lesbians don't fuck around. They wash each other's underwear and have long discussions about their ex-lovers. Lesbian sex has been a big disappointment, I can tell you."

"Then why are you a lesbian?"

"Because men are boring out of bed. And because I like women's bodies. I want to like my own. I want to *understand* my own." Miko put down her delicate cup. "Before Nicky," she said, "I'd been celibate for two years."

"You? I thought you had a carnal knowledge of almost every lesbian in Seattle."

"It's hard for me to have a relationship," Miko said. "At bottom I'm scared of being pushed around like my mother was. Maybe I'm afraid of love, maybe I make art instead of love. If I'm provocative it's to scare myself out of shyness, to challenge myself, to show myself I'm not shocked by bodies or sexuality. I think I was attracted to Nicky because she was so willing to explore her own sexuality in a way that terrifies me."

"Did she really say she wanted to leave Oak?"

"Yes, she did. It may have only been because she wanted to seduce me, but it *felt* real. She said she was starting to feel bored with the sameness of sex with Oak and that even though they'd both had other lovers, she always felt she was more into non-monogamy than Oak. She thought Oak was beginning to get too possessive."

"Do you believe her? Or do you believe Oak?"

"I don't know anymore," said Miko. "I probably just believed what I wanted to believe."

I got up to leave. The shaded light in the room was very lovely, falling on the many images and art books. Miko's studio was like an elaborate, rose-tinted carapace that she had built around herself.

"About Hadley," Miko said, looking up at me. "I did want to sleep with her."

"I know."

"But you two don't have that kind of relationship."

"No," I said. "We don't."

"You're not mad at me then? I was only checking."

"I'm not mad," I said. "It's okay to check. Maybe someday it will be all right. It's not now, that's all."

Miko smiled at me. "So—I'll take a look at these reels tomorrow and give you a call. Any chance you could come over to the office if I find something?"

"Of course."

The next afternoon I sat with Miko in a small cubbyhole in a building belonging to the Seattle School District, watching three twenty-minute porn videos made circa 1970. They were blurred black and white and in very bad condition.

"Probably because they're copies," said Miko. "With this kind of video you get real reproduction problems."

The first reel showed a very young Nicky with long curly hair and a firm body stripping down to her bra and underpants and then wandering around the room, at first looking at herself in the mirror and then very self-consciously lying down on the bed spread-eagled and starting to touch herself. There was no editing to the video and everything took place in real time. Finally the door opened and a man I didn't recognize came in. With considerable nervousness the two of them pretended to have a conversation. Nicky couldn't help giggling and looking off camera. In response to some unheard direction the man pulled down his jeans and lay down on the bed. The camera caught his erect penis just before Nicky straddled him. They bounced up and down a few times and then the video ended.

"Not too much foreplay," Miko commented. "I think you'll be more interested in the next one."

It looked like the same bed. Nicky was sitting on it cross-legged, smoking a joint, when the door opened and Hanna came in. Both of them were only wearing bikini underpants.

179

"I think the director must have had them start without clothes so they could cram more action into the short amount of time they had," Miko said, adding, "It's hard seeing Nicky, knowing she's really dead."

I was fascinated. Hanna didn't seem half so nervous or silly as Nicky. Lithe and blond, she advanced right into the room and gracefully seated herself on the bed. Nicky handed her the joint.

Tentatively the two women, who couldn't have been more than eighteen or nineteen, touched each other's breasts. Nicky was still receiving a lot of encouragement from off-camera. Hanna looked strangely self-confident. Perhaps she thought of it as another role. Maybe she was stoned.

Hanna began to take the initiative. She took Nicky's small breast in her mouth and began to pull Nicky's underpants down. The door opened and a very sweet and guilty-looking young man came in. David Gustafson.

"Oh, my god," I said.

He had long hair and a tie-dyed shirt and bell bottoms. He too was smoking a joint and trying to look cool. The two women were supposed to be too occupied to notice, but of course eventually they did and invited him to join them.

"This is really feeble," I said. "Every man's fantasy of lesbianism—a couple of chicks just waiting for a guy."

Miko gave me an amused look. "Then you'll love the third one."

"I can hardly wait to see Loie," I said.

The third one began where the second left off, with Nicky, Hanna and David in bed. First Nicky and David did it, then David and Hanna. I waited for the ubiquitous door to open. Who was Loie going to fuck? Would it be her cousin or husband-to-be or Nicky? Or all three?

Then it all went fuzzy and pale. You could see the door open, and someone come in. It was probably a woman because it looked like long hair, but then again it could have been a man in those days. The ghost joined the others in a

180

wispy white mingling and then the video ended.

"Oh no," I said. "I wanted to see Loie."

"How do you know it was Loie?"

"Of course it was," I said. "That's the point. That they were all in these films together."

"I don't know," said Miko. "I suppose I've been wondering if Loie might not have directed them. She might have borrowed the Portapak from the drama department and talked her cousin and Nicky and David into a wild afternoon."

"But if Loie wasn't in the video why would Nicky say she was?"

"That was our construction," Miko said. "All Nicky told Oak is that she'd made a porn film with Loie. We assumed that meant a professional or semi-professional film with Loie. But it could have been Loie who made the video. That might account for Nicky calling her a hypocrite. If Loie had been *in* the video rather than orchestrating it then Nicky might have tried to protect her, like she did Hanna."

I wasn't convinced. "It could have been the man in the first video who was shooting them. I wonder who he was?"

Miko nodded. "It's also possible that Loie changed the light setting somehow—deliberately—so that her part wouldn't be visible."

"I wonder if Hanna and David know these tapes still exist?"

Miko shook her head. "That's the frightening thing about committing youthful indiscretions in front of a camera," she said. "I had a girlfriend who posed for *Playboy* when she was eighteen. She still worries, twenty years later, about those photos popping up sometime."

"But these are hardly hardcore," I said. "Why would any of them worry about little videos like this destroying their reputation?"

"Maybe they didn't remember very well what they'd done on camera. Sometimes things have a way of getting worse in your memory."

It still puzzled me. Obviously the person who would have been hurt the most by these was Loie. And she was dead.

When I got home that evening, Hadley was in the living room watching the sunset out the window with her feet up on the coffee table.

"Gracie called," Hadley said without moving. "No message. Again."

"I wonder what she wants?" I said, going to the phone. "I know now she hasn't taken Loie's manuscript or notes. I don't know what else she could be calling about."

Hadley didn't say anything.

This time I reached her.

"Oh hello," she said. "We finally connect. How are you?"

"Fine," I said. "Ah, how are you?"

"Oh, I'm fine," she said, and paused.

"Did you have something to tell me?" I asked her, for the first time wondering if I should have shut the door to the bedroom.

"Well not exactly tell you," Gracie laughed in her husky voice. "More to ask you—I wonder if you're interested in going to a movie tomorrow night?"

"Oh," I said. To give myself time I called into the other room, "Hadley, are we doing anything tomorrow night?"

"I have to work until nine," she said neutrally.

"Oh. Ah. Yes," I told Gracie. "That would be fine, that would be nice."

"Great," she said, and told me about the various films in town. While we discussed the options available I tried desperately to assure myself that there was nothing strange about this, it was perfectly normal, I went to films with friends all the time.

We agreed to meet at the Harvard Exit and said good-bye.

"That was Gracie," I said brightly, coming into the living room. "We're going to go to the early movie tomorrow night. It's an Eric Rohmer film."

Hadley gave me a sardonic look. "Well, that's nice."

"Yes," I said. "I'm sure it will be."

19

IF HERCULE POIROT COULD carry it off, why couldn't I? I called up seven people on Saturday and asked them to stop by Sunday evening for coffee and dessert. I thought David and Sonya were going to be the hardest, but Sonya was perfectly agreeable.

"Oh, are you still in town, Randy?" she asked. "Of course, David and I would be delighted to stop in. Are you sure you wouldn't like to go to church with us in the morning?"

I hastily declined with a not very convincing excuse about my relative's health, and I gave her directions. Eight o'clock would be fine. I hoped as I hung up that it hadn't occurred to David to check my story in Southern California.

Hanna I convinced by saying that I'd been thinking over our discussion and I'd come up with some new fundraising ideas. She said she could only come after eight o'clock, closer to eight fifteen or twenty, and I said that was fine. It would be no good if she and David met in the parking lot at the top of the hill.

I told Mrs. Marsh I had some photos of my grandfather

and his relatives that I hoped she could help me identify. I purposefully didn't invite her mother, just in case things got a little rough, but Edith assumed I had and said they'd both love to visit.

I told Miko I'd like to get to know her better and I told Oak the same thing.

Oak sounded skeptical, but agreed to come anyway. She was curious about the videos if nothing else.

Hadley said she couldn't get off until nine because Doreen was still ill but I told her that was all right. She could help me pick up the pieces.

Everything seemed set until Penny called up and asked if she could drop Antonia off at nine Sunday morning instead of ten as we'd previously agreed. I had forgotten we'd agreed any such thing.

"Where exactly are you going again?" I asked, stalling.

"To that all-day meeting in Bellingham," she said, her voice rising. "I *told* you about it ages ago."

"Oh, right," I said. "Well, I don't mind when you drop Antonia off, but you've got to pick her up no later than seven o'clock."

"Pam," she said. "That's not what we agreed. The meeting isn't over until five and then we were going to eat dinner with Tom and Martha and it's an hour and half drive back. . . . "

"I forgot I'd invited people over," I said. "It can't be helped."

"Can't Hadley. . . ?"

"No, there's a lot of flu around, she's got to fill in until nine."

"Well, you shouldn't have offered unless you really meant it." Penny's voice was sharp.

"I *did* really mean it. I'm happy to take care of Antonia *all day*. But if you're going to be any later than seven you'll need to get a paid baby sitter."

"A baby sitter!" she gasped as if I'd said paid child molester.

We argued for another ten minutes. Finally I agreed to take Antonia at eight-thirty in the morning and Penny said she'd pick her up no later than seven-thirty that night.

I was glad Hadley was working and couldn't see me getting ready for the film with Gracie. I took a long bath, moussed my hair and put on my special red-and-white-striped shirt with my straight-legged black jeans. Then I drove off to the Harvard Exit on Capitol Hill.

Gracie met me in the lobby that was more like a drawing room with drapes, settees and a piano. It looked as if she too had dressed up a little. She was wearing a big mohair pullover in shades of peach and rhubarb over honey-colored wool slacks. Her cheeks were pink and her salt and pepper hair curled forward above her direct brown eyes.

She gave me a kiss on the cheek. I blushed even as I thought, surely she knows about Hadley. Surely June has told her.

I'd thought a movie was a fairly safe thing to do with a woman you liked but whom you didn't want to get any wrong ideas. Still, that eighty or ninety minutes felt very long. I like Eric Rohmer, but I don't remember much about the film, except that it was part of a series appropriately titled, "Comedies and Proverbs." I was acutely conscious of Gracie's perfume, of the sensation of her body next to mine. I experienced slightly dizzy feelings of lust that I hadn't for a long time, and I lost myself in hopeless reasonings: Maybe Hadley had been right, maybe we shouldn't settle down. Staying together in a houseboat was fun, but it wasn't real life. If I could feel this way about another woman then maybe I wasn't ready for long-term fidelity. I hadn't had enough experience as a lesbian... for instance, I'd never been with a woman so much older, so much more sophisticated.

After the film we walked down to the B & O, a local cafe, and had decaf espressos and sour cream lemon pie. I couldn't decide whether my disloyalty was to Hadley or to the Espressomat. Still, it was nice to be somewhere out of range of political lesbians and washing machines for a while.

"I suppose there's no doubt that Pauline killed Loie and Nicky?" Gracie asked.

"I suppose not. The newspaper said the means of death was the same in both cases, and Pauline *did* take the manuscript. Still, I have some questions."

"It would be interesting if you turned up some new evidence," Gracie said. "An investigation must be like writing a book, that's how I imagine it. You've got to do your research, your interviews, follow up your leads, learn the historical background, put the ideas into context, firm up your arguments and present your case."

"I could never write a book like that," I said, a little enviously. "Mine would be full of dead ends, tentative conclusions, backpedaling, outright wrong assumptions. I no sooner have one idea than another sounds better. I would have had a hell of a time if I'd actually had to write my thesis on the Seattle General Strike. I loved doing the research, but I would have been hopeless at making my argument stick. Ever since junior high English the favorite criticism of my teachers was, 'Pamela Nilsen, where *is* the topic sentence in this paragraph?'"

"Anybody can come up with a single point of view and push it to death," Gracie said charitably. "Most of us were willing students of the one topic sentence school of thought. Which is probably why feminist political writing is so boring to read. The thesis comes first and then the examples are modified to fit the thesis. Any fact that doesn't fit is thrown out. Take, for example, one of the most famous catch phrases of the movement: 'Pornography is the theory; rape is the practice.' It sounds great, but what does it actually mean?"

"It's supposed to get people—women—angry," I said. "If you just sit around discussing the ambiguities of each subject, you never get anything to change. Like in South

Africa, it's maybe okay to point out the irony of necklacing, of blacks killing blacks, but what you really want is the overthrow of white rule there."

"I'm the last person to dispute that," Gracie shook her head. "And I take your point. I'm sure you and I want an end to the sexual exploitation of women as much as Loie Marsh did. But what's come to interest me increasingly is the *methods* used to effect change, as well as the nature of power itself. Democracy works through pluralism, through individuals and interest groups listening to each other and figuring out ways of co-existing. The feminist movement is so polarized that no one is *listening* anymore. All we seem to be able to do is repeat ourselves endlessly."

"Is it really that hopeless?"

"Yes—and the most impossible thing about it all is that everyone is using their own sexuality as a reference point. They don't say they are, but they are underneath."

"It *has* to be legitimate for a woman who's been raped or abused to say that porn is frightening and disgusting to her, that she wants to live her life without it, in safety."

"But it also has to be all right for a woman who wants to explore her sexuality to do so without mass feminist disapproval."

"I don't know," I said, shaking my head and thinking of Loie, "We can only speak for ourselves, yet everyone would rather speak for everyone *but* themselves."

Gracie laughed, "So all we can write now is our autobiographies? No more theory, no more criticism, no more polemics?"

"Not if theorizing is an excuse never to deal with your own sexuality."

"Does that mean me too?" Gracie asked in an insinuating tone.

I blushed slightly and tried for a lighter tone. "I wonder how people in twenty or fifty years will look back on this time? Will the anger seem incomprehensible, will people be more comfortable with their sexual identity, will there be new sexual identities, will sex seem less important?

It certainly can't get more important."

"I doubt it will ever not be important," said Gracie, touching my arm slightly as we got up to leave. "But maybe what other people do with their bodies won't be quite as highly charged a topic as it is now. When the rainforests are gone and the polluted ocean has flooded downtown Seattle and we're all living on top of Queen Anne Hill in bunkers to protect us from the ultra-violet rays, we'll look back and say, 'And we were arguing about pictures of naked people!'"

We went out into the night and the October air was crisp and soft at the same time. For a moment I felt an overwhelming gratitude that the world hadn't ended or changed irrevocably while we'd been inside the B & O eating sour cream lemon pie.

Then Gracie asked, "How long have you been a lesbian?" and I was back to heart-thudding sweet panic.

"Not long," I said.

"Me either," she said. "Only ten years."

"Ten years," I said. "That's long."

"Not if you put in a good thirty being heterosexual before that. I'm still not always sure where to begin." She took my arm.

"Gracie, Gracie, I should tell you. I'm involved with Hadley."

"I know. June told me."

"So you just want to be friends, right?" I felt relief—and a slight disappointment.

"Not exactly. But I'd accept that," she added.

I wanted to ask, Why me? Why are you interested in me? I'm not an intellectual—I've never read Lacan—or Foucault. I've never been to New York and about the only place I've been in Europe is the Hardanger Vidda in Norway.

Then Gracie's hand moved up my arm to my shoulder. "There's something very attractive about you, Pam."

"There is?" I quavered. And added in a deeper voice, "I like you too."

She stopped me away from the streetlight and gave me a kiss. Her lips were firm and cool and tasted of lemon. "Something to remember me by," she said.

"I'll remember," I said.

Hadley was watching TV when I came in.

"Gracie says hi," I chirped.

Hadley grunted.

For some reason a wave of affection for her traveled through me. I liked her long body and her easy ways, her Texas accent, her funny smile. I liked her better than anybody I knew. Good old Hadley.

I sat down beside her and together we watched the end of *Sunset Boulevard*.

Far too early the next morning Penny and Ray appeared with Antonia. The anxious parents loaded us with soft toys, expressed milk, formula and advice before setting off to Bellingham for a meeting of Washingtonians Against Contra Aid.

"It'll be more fun when she's older," I said sleepily, watching Hadley cradle Antonia in her arms, all the while looking into her tiny face and making cooing noises.

"Oh Pam, it's fun *now*. You just lack the maternal instinct."

"Probably," I agreed, and went off to the Canal Market to buy the Sunday paper and some croissants for breakfast.

But at noon Hadley went off to the Espressomat to "check on her patients," as she said, and I was left in charge of Baby A. After an all too brief half hour of fun and games with me and her baby rabbit, it was two hours of tears, followed by a brief nap and then an interminable quarrelsome period, neither smiles nor tears, just relentless unhappy noises.

I walked her up and down. I tried to interest her in her

190

toys. "Hey, what about this rabbit?" I said. "Nice rabbit, Baby A." I told her stories and sang her songs. I said, "I don't look *that* different from your mom, give me a break."

Still, she whined. Finally I felt so exhausted that I simply lay down on the couch with her on my chest and said, "We're resting now. And that's that."

We both fell asleep.

I woke to the sound of footsteps coming quietly down the long dock. It had gotten darker and begun to storm while Antonia and I were sleeping. Rain lashed the picture windows and the rowboat knocked against the dock. For a moment I panicked. What if this was one of my guests already? I hadn't had a chance to make coffee, much less prepare myself emotionally. Then I looked at my watch and saw it was only seven o'clock. Thank god, Penny had gotten back early. I carefully placed Antonia on the couch and got up to meet her.

But as I moved through the darkened houseboat to the side door I caught a glimpse of the figure through the window. It wasn't Penny.

It was someone wearing a cap and a jacket. He or she was moving steathily along the wall of the houseboat and in his or her hand dangled a long length of something.

Okay, I said to myself. Breathe deeply. Remember to throw your whole body into your kick and block. Now's your chance to practice what you've learned. You have the advantage; it's dim and they can't see you. They don't even know you're here. You can just push them into the water and call the police.

At that moment, Antonia began to shriek.

We'd never discussed what to do in my self-defense class if you happened to have a thirteen-week-old baby on your hands.

"Shhh," I whispered.

The footsteps stopped at the side door and a hand turned the knob. There was no way I could get from this end of the houseboat to the other end, where the kitchen door led to the back deck and to the stairs up the hillside. Not fast enough, and not with Antonia. So I did the next best thing. I grabbed Antonia and slipped out the glass door to the deck facing Portage Bay, just as whoever it was came in the house.

Unfortunately I realized as the driving rain and wind slammed the door shut behind me that this was the door that automatically locked. The intruder had seen me silhouetted against the glass and had gone out again, blocking the side deck and the way to the stairs. He or she was still unrecognizable, but moving quickly.

I did the only thing that occurred to me: clutching Antonia I jumped into the rowboat, slipped off the knot that held it fastened to the deck and floated off into the dark water.

"Don't tell your mother about this," I said, as Antonia sputtered, too surprised to cry. "Just sit there and I'll get us out of this."

Why weren't there any oars in this fucking boat? Then I remembered. Hadley had taken them out to revarnish them yesterday. The wind was blowing in more than gusts and a alarmingly strong current seemed to be taking us quickly away from shore. The rain came down like needles.

"Help," I shouted, but no one came out of their houseboat. We must be already too far out to be heard. I saw the figure on the deck hesitate a moment, then slide the canoe, which *did* have paddles, into the water, get in and begin to paddle out to us.

I wished I could believe that whoever it was sincerely wanted to help me and Antonia.

There was nowhere to go and nothing to do but wait. I couldn't hide. The rain poured down and the waves swirled us out into the dark bay. No boats were out tonight, the weather was too bad. The houseboats along the shore rocked eerily. I could barely see, my glasses were useless in the rain. I began to shiver. The wind was cold out here and in a sweatshirt, jeans and no shoes I wasn't prepared for this, nor was Antonia, in her little blue sleeper. I'd grabbed her blanket but that wouldn't keep her warm or dry for long.

"Oh baby," I said. I hugged her close to me and suddenly my fear passed and I felt terribly angry. No one was going hurt Antonia if I could help it.

The paddling was swift, if unprofessional. As the canoe came nearer I saw it was a woman, a tall woman with her hair hidden under a cap.

"Hanna!" I shouted desperately. "Listen, Hanna. I never wished you any harm. I can understand why you felt afraid of Loie and Nicky telling people what they knew about you. But listen—Hanna. Please! You can't keep killing people. You've got to stop sometime. Too many people know. You can't kill all of them—so what's the point of killing me?"

The woman stopped paddling, as if she were thinking, then in a sudden furious burst she was alongside. The tallness and slenderness were the same, but the nose was quite different.

"Sonya!" I said.

I know she wasn't thinking. There were so many things she could have done: knocked me out with a paddle, overturned my boat. Only a desperate person would have sprung out of the canoe at me. She landed at one end of the rowboat. I put Antonia down and she let out a wail of complete indignation. Sonya and I grappled. Her strong ugly face was contorted with emotion and she was breathing furiously. I felt her vicious grip around my neck and all of a sudden I remembered what to do. We'd broken a lot of chokes in my class. I poked Sonya in the eye, flung her arms sideways and flipped her sideways—out of the boat, into the water.

Unfortunately I lost my balance too and plunged head-first after her.

The first thing I heard when I surfaced was Antonia wailing. Then a hand pushed my head back under the icy water. I lunged for the rowboat, choking on water. The hand pushed my head down again, long enough so that I began to lose consciousness. With every ounce of strength I had left I grabbed on to the rowboat, brought my feet up to my chest and kicked out. I caught her right in the windpipe.

I heard her suck in water and go down. I hauled myself up the side of the boat. Antonia was still crying. Sonya flailed helplessly out of reach.

Was Sonya going to drown? Should I let her?

Like a pair of otters, two women kayakers were upon us.

"Is that a *baby* crying?" one asked, even as the other was extending a paddle to Sonya.

"Yes," I gasped. "This woman has just been trying to kill us."

20

An hour later, still damp and chilled, I sat in the living room of the houseboat with Miko, Oak, Edith Marsh, Mrs. Sandbakker, Hanna, Penny, Ray, Hadley and a cop, trying to explain what had happened. One of the kayakers had testified she saw Sonya leap at me, and the police had found a leash and a dog collar on the floating dock. Sonya must have dropped them when she jumped into the canoe.

The police had gotten there sooner than I'd had any right to expect. I still didn't know why but they'd immediately believed my story over Sonya's protests that it had been me trying to drown her, that she'd only been acting in self-defense. Two cops had taken her, wet and hysterical, off in their squad car, while the third cop had stayed to get our statements.

"I thought it might be someone in the videos," I said. "But I believed it was probably Hanna. I thought the only way to get the truth out of her was to get everyone here and have a confrontational scene. I've seen you on stage, Hanna, you don't crack when you're playing a part, only when you can't keep it up any longer. I thought seeing David again would do it."

"Why didn't you suspect David or Sonya?" asked Hanna. Her voice was mild, considering that I'd just said I'd believed her capable of murdering two people. She sounded interested in the fact, as if talking with a director about her interpretation of a play.

"I did suspect David, but I also didn't think his feelings about Loie ran as strong as yours. After all, he hadn't seen Loie for years. As for Sonya—I realize now she was the woman in the video, the ghostly one. But even if I'd seen her I suppose I wouldn't have thought she'd kill Loie and Nicky because of it. She was afraid that Loie was going to say something on the panel."

"How could Loie think that was going to help the cause against pornography?" Penny asked. She was beginning to look more normal now, after the shock of coming home to the houseboat to find, first, no one there and then, her dripping sister clutching a very unhappy baby driven up in a police car. The baby in question was sleeping an exhausted sleep on the lap of her father.

"She told me when she came to Seattle that her book was going to expose the damage that porn did to people," Hanna said. "I said I'd sue her if she mentioned me. But it was the... family stuff I was worried about. Knowing Loie she would have made a big deal about it. The video tapes I could have dealt with I guess." She shuddered a little. "Though it pissed me off that as usual Loie wasn't actually in the scenario, but somewhere outside, in this case directing."

"Then it wasn't you at the conference trying to talk Loie out of her confessions?" I asked.

"Nicky was the one who tried to talk to Loie and warn her against making the past public," Oak said. "She told me during dinner, she said Loie was as pig-headed as ever."

"So Loie told Nicky that she was going to talk about the video. And who did Nicky tell?" Hadley asked.

I remembered back to the conference, to Nicky talking to someone outside the auditorium. "Sonya," I said. "The person she joked was trying to save her." Sonya must have come inside with the crowd after Gracie's speech. It was all starting to fit together now.

"It was Sonya in the audience who Loie saw," I continued. "Sonya who made a date with Loie on campus before the evening panel. She must have gotten the idea of strangling Loie with a leash from Nicky. She saw Nicky take off of the dog collar when they were talking and put it in her jacket pocket. She followed Nicky to the Ethiopian restaurant and stole the dog collar and leash from the jacket, got back in time to surprise Loie by throwing the leash around her neck and strangling her."

"Didn't Nicky realize that Sonya had murdered Loie?" Hadley asked Oak.

"I think she suspected Sonya," said Oak. "But it was her dog collar that was used. She didn't want to get dragged into it."

"How could Nicky have thought she was safe from Sonya?" Hanna wondered. "We knew what Sonya was like way back then. Willing to wait for what she wanted, but ruthless somehow. She wanted David and when Loie left him she was there to pick up the pieces."

Oak couldn't help it, she began to cry. "Then that was why Nicky had to die? Just because Sonya worried Nicky might connect Loie's murder to *her*?"

"There's something I never thought to mention," said Miko. "Sonya was at my workshop. That's when she first saw Nicky with the dog collar and leash. Maybe that's where the notion came of making it look like Loie's murder was done by someone into S/M."

"Sonya must have also heard Nicky denounce Clea Florence," I said. "And realized that Nicky was capable of denouncing her."

"What I can't forgive myself for is putting you in danger, Pam," said Hadley. "Last night when Sonya called and asked for Randy Potter I told her she had a wrong number. She got quite interested when she heard it was the Hadley Harper/Pam Nilsen residence."

197

"But how could she have known who I was?"

"I told her, I'm afraid," said Edith Marsh. "I called Sonya to thank them for the wreath. I'm afraid I said something about being invited to Pam Nilsen's on Sunday evening for coffee. I said you'd been very supportive around Loie's death... There's something else I must confess," she added and looked ashamed, "I lied when I said I'd called Pauline Saturday night after Loie died. I didn't want her to come to the service. Later it didn't seem to matter that I hadn't called her."

"So David probably didn't know anything about this," said Hanna. "That's not surprising, I guess. He was always so passive."

"No," said Mrs. Sandbakker, "you're wrong that he didn't suspect. Just before we were leaving tonight for Pam's, I got a phone call from David. We'd kept in touch from time to time ever since the early days. He wanted to tell me that Sonya had told him she was planning to meet Loie just before the panel discussion to discuss the possibility of forming a coalition to pass an anti-pornography bill in Bellevue. Afterwards Sonya said that Loie hadn't come to their meeting. David hadn't questioned her, but he was worried. And when Nicky was murdered he began to think that Sonya might have had something to do with both deaths. He told me on the phone that Sonya had insisted on going to this woman Randy Potter's alone. He feared the worst. He wanted to call the police but he couldn't do it to his own wife. He asked me to call them. I did."

"I thought it was too much of a coincidence that two squad cars just happened to be cruising along Fuhrman Ave," Hadley said.

"Sonya must have felt the net closing in," I said. "She'd killed twice to protect her secret, and she was ready to kill again."

"She didn't know that you couldn't even see her on the video," said Miko. "That's the irony."

"What I don't understand," said the cop to me, "is what you thought you were doing, getting everybody you suspected here like this. Didn't you know that at least one of them might be dangerous? Why didn't you call the police?"

"The police had their suspect," I said. "I didn't think I'd convince you unless I had a confession that had been witnessed by a whole group of people. And anyway," I said. "Hercule Poirot did it. Lots of times."

It was one of those fall days when the weather actually seems better than spring or summer. Spring may be exciting and summer may be luxurious, but at no time other than October is there such a feeling of fullness and completion. The leaves were falling thick and fast but the trees showed hardly any sign of diminishing. All around us were fiery maples and golden horse chestnuts and they blazed against the china blue sky. The scent of the sun on dry leaves was intoxicating.

"Look Toni, a leaf," I said, holding up an especially fine specimen of a burgundy-colored Japanese maple.

She reached for it eagerly and took hold of it with that curiously tenacious baby grip of hers. I'd been spending more time with my niece and the strength of her tiny fingers was familiar to me, especially when it involved my hair.

"I think she wants to eat it," Penny remarked. "Get that out of your mouth, dear."

We were sitting by the side of our parents' grave at the cemetery not far from the family house. It was so near we hadn't been here for exactly five years, not since the day of the funeral.

Sig and Louise Nilsen. Born in Seattle in the thirties, died in Seattle in the eighties. They had both attended Ballard High, then Louise had gone to secretarial school while Sig had gone to fight in Korea. He'd written Louise letters home, letters we still had, that always started out, "My darling honey." They'd lived through the economic boom of the sixties, built their printing business up, bought an older house and fixed it up, raised twin daughters and seen them through college and part of graduate school.

They would have seen a lot more if they'd lived, and maybe they wouldn't have liked some of it. Maybe they would have, though. I'd never know.

"I loved the way Dad would make us popcorn and read us stories on the nights Mom went to her weaving class," Penny said.

"He helped me get my bike back once after Joey Perkins at school made me give it to him after losing a bet. And he never even yelled at me."

"We complained about the print shop, but I used to love going down there and playing."

"Remember when Mom first showed us how to run the little Multilith? How everybody at school was jealous of us because we printed the class newsletter ourselves."

"I think they were happy together," said Penny. "If they had to go, maybe it's better they went together. They hardly ever used to fight—they were very... harmonious somehow."

"Except that one time, remember? When she locked him out of the house?"

"And we kept asking, Are you going to get a divorce? I think we'd just seen Hayley Mills in *The Parent Trap* and thought we might be separated, one with each parent."

"You would have gone with Dad," I said without rancor.

"You were Mom's favorite."

"I'd have liked to have known Dad better."

Penny nodded; she couldn't speak for a moment. Then she took Antonia in her arms and said, almost fiercely, "We should have done this a long time ago. Come up here, I mean."

"Yes," I said. "It's time we started remembering."

The fall leaves swirled around us and were gone almost

before they touched the earth. But Antonia, who had her whole life before her, held out her hands and laughed delightedly.

Six weeks later, in early December, when the leaves that had seemed as if they would never fall from their branches had practically vanished, Hadley and I had our housewarming.

"Houses-warming," Hadley said, though that was something of a moot point. It was both one house and two.

In the course of her real estate search, Hadley had run into a house in the Wallingford district that had been divided into upper and lower apartments. We decided to buy it together and to live separately.

That didn't in the end turn out to be such a hard decision. It was harder to decide who was going to live where. "If you wouldn't keep calling it 'top' and 'bottom'," Hadley said, "it would be easier."

"Just think of it as a flow of energy," I said.

"Yeah, from the downstairs to the upstairs. Upstairs apartments are always cheaper to heat."

We compromised by agreeing to share the utilities and I took the upstairs with its view of Lake Union. Hadley got the downstairs deck surrounded by rose bushes.

"No loud parties now," Hadley warned.

We had separate mailboxes, separate telephones and separate entrances, none of which were, of course, proof against spying. Still, they did offer a small buffer against too much togetherness.

"Nice!" Miko said when she turned up at the housewarming. She had brought each of us a small Japanese print. Hadley's was a chaste landscape, but mine showed a woman masturbating with a mirror in one hand. I had to admit I found it somewhat arousing, "But where will I put it?" I wondered, already thinking of Antonia coming to visit.

"Pam, you're hopeless," Miko said, giving me an affectionate hug.

Ray and Penny gave me a saucepan set and Hadley an iron. "Weren't these wedding presents to them?" I asked Hadley suspiciously.

"Now, now," said Hadley. "This is the nearest *we'll* get to a wedding, I can tell you."

It was a little bit like the wedding reception two months ago. Not as many old neighbors and relatives, but more of the people we counted as friends and family. Moe and Allen, June and Eddy, Beth and Janis, all the employees of the Espressomat, looking in radiant health for once. Elizabeth, newly delivered of a baby boy, was there with her lover Nan and the rest of their children. She and Ray stood around having an animated talk about daycare in more advanced countries.

Penny was dancing with Allen; Hadley was dancing with June; Hanna was dancing with Eddy.

I drifted out to the deck in back and Gracie London followed me. She was looking fabulous in a green silk shirt and viridian copper earrings, but we met as friends, nothing more.

"You never told me you were so close to solving Loie and Nicky's murders!" she exclaimed. "One minute we're drinking coffee at the B & O and the next you're fighting a sea battle in Portage Bay from what I hear."

"I didn't really solve the murder," I said, with more honesty than modesty. "It's my old problem of making the final argument I suppose. I can't summarize and resolve things. The nearest I seem to get is making everyone so nervous with my questions that I precipitate events. I admit, I really never took Sonya seriously. She was so well-groomed! I should have remembered she believed in direct action."

Gracie laughed. "Have your ideas about porn have changed since all this?"

I had to think. "I guess," I said slowly. "I'm not so ready to judge as I once was. In the first place I hardly even knew what porn was or how people felt about it. It used to be a monolithic subject. There was porn and there was no porn, kind of like matter and anti-matter, and either you liked it or you didn't. Either you thought it should be abolished or you thought it should be sold everywhere. There wasn't room for contradiction, for your own contradictory feelings. But Loie Marsh's idea of porn wasn't David Gustafson's or Nicky Kay's. My idea of porn isn't yours and yours isn't Miko's."

"What *is* yours?" Gracie asked.

"I'm probably going to spend the rest of my life finding out. And once I've figured it out it will probably change again. All I know is you can't speak for anyone else. And you can't let anyone speak for you."

"Well, I think that there has to be a lot more talking about it—or no more talking," Gracie said.

"I want a two-year moratorium while I fundraise for Nicaraguan ambulances and learn how to sea kayak," I said. "I think I'm kind of talked out for a while."

"What kind of a feminist are you?" said Gracie. "You can't be talked-*out*!"

But I was listening to the music from within the house. It was something wild and wonderful from a place in the world where they knew how to get down and enjoy themselves. It had heavy drums and a sax like a ripcord and a voice that shouted seductively through the rhythm, rich and gravelly.

Hadley was in the middle of a seething mass of bodies, rocking like a crazy fool. From across the room she saw me and grinned.

"Hey neighbor," she called. "Want to dance?"

About the Author

Barbara Wilson is the author of two other mysteries featuring Pam Nilsen (*Murder in the Collective* and *Sisters of the Road*). With *Gaudí Afternoon*, she introduced Cassandra Reilly. A second Cassandra Reilly mystery, *Trouble in Transylvania*, will be published in 1993. Barbara Wilson is also the author of two novels, *Cows and Horses* and *Ambitious Women*, and the short story collection *Miss Venezuela*. She has translated the work of Cora Sandel and Ebba Haslund from Norwegian. She lives in Seattle and is co-publisher of Seal Press.

SELECTED MYSTERIES FROM SEAL PRESS

MURDER IN THE COLLECTIVE by Barbara Wilson. $9.95, 1-878067-23-0. This riveting feminist murder mystery featuring Seattle sleuth Pam Nilsen is set against a background of political intrigue. First in the Series.

SISTERS OF THE ROAD by Barbara Wilson. $9.95, 1-878067-24-9. Pam Nilsen is back again, this time looking for teenaged Trish Margolin—and the murderer of Trish's best friend—in a suspenseful psychological thriller that probes the issues of prostitution and violence against women. Second in the series.

GAUDÍ AFTERNOON by Barbara Wilson. $8.95, 1-878067-89-X. Amidst the dream-like architecture of Gaudí's city, this high-spirited comic thriller introduces amateur sleuth Cassandra Reilly as she chases people of all genders and motives.

LADIES' NIGHT by Elisabeth Bowers. $8.95, 0-931188-65-2. Meg Lacey, divorced mother and savvy P.I., tackles a child pornography and prostitution ring that inhabits the back alleys and nightclubs of Vancouver, B.C. First in the series.

NO FORWARDING ADDRESS by Elisabeth Bowers. $18.95, 1-878067-13-3. Meg Lacey is back on the streets of Vancouver in search of a missing wife but soon becomes embroiled in a web of family secrets—and a puzzle far more deadly than she ever expected. Second in the series.

HALLOWED MURDER by Ellen Hart. $8.95, 0-931188-83-0 Featuring a memorable cast of characters including Minnesota restaurateur—and part-time sleuth—Jane Lawless, this suspenseful mystery gives an intriguing inside view of the undercurrents of sorority and religious life.

VITAL LIES by Ellen Hart. $8.95, 1-878067-02-8 Jane Lawless and her unpredictable sidekick, Cordelia Thorn, unravel a gripping story of buried memories from the past that wreak havoc on the present.

GLORY DAYS by Rosie Scott, $8.95, 1-878067-72-5 Glory Day, streetwise artist, nightclub singer and uncommon heroine, makes her debut in this dazzling thriller from New Zealand.

SEAL PRESS, founded in 1976 to provide a forum for women writers and feminist issues, has many other books of fiction, non-fiction and poetry. You may order directly from us at 3131 Western Avenue, Suite 410, Seattle, Washington 98121 (add 15% of total book order for shipping and handling). Write to us for a free catalog or if you would like to be on our mailing list.